FROM THE LAND
OF THE MOON

Milena Agus

FROM THE LAND OF THE MOON

*Translated from the Italian
by Ann Goldstein*

Europa
editions

Europa Editions
116 East 16th Street
New York, N.Y. 10003
www.europaeditions.com
info@europaeditions.com

Copyright © 2006 by Nottetempo Srl.
First Publication 2011 by Europa Editions
Second printing, 2011

Translation by Ann Goldstein
Original Title: *Mal di pietre*
Translation copyright © 2010 by Europa Editions

Library of Congress Cataloging in Publication Data is available
ISBN 978-1-60945-001-4

Agus, Milena
From the Land of the Moon

Winner of the Zerilli-Marimò/City of Rome Prize
for Italian Fiction 2006.
This translation was made possible thanks to kind support
from the Zerilli-Marimò/City of Rome Prize fund.

Book design by Emanuele Ragnisco
www.mekkanografici.com
Cover photo: Ignazietta Lentino

Prepress by Grafica Punto Print – Rome

Printed in Canada

"If I never meet you in this life, let me feel the lack."
—Soldier in *The Thin Red Line*

FROM THE LAND
OF THE MOON

1.

Grandmother met the Veteran in the fall of 1950. She had come from Cagliari to the mainland for the first time. She must have been around forty, and had no children, because *su mali de is perdas*—her kidney stones—always caused her to miscarry in the first months. So, with her sack-like overcoat and high, laced shoes and the suitcase her husband had brought as an evacuee to her village, she was sent to the thermal baths to be cured.

2.

She had married late, in June of 1943, after the American bombing of Cagliari, and in those days to be thirty and not yet settled was already to be something of an old maid. Not that she was ugly, or lacked suitors—on the contrary. But at a certain point the wooers called less frequently and then stopped, each time before they had officially asked my great-grandfather for her hand. Dear *signorina*, circumstances beyond my control prevent me from calling on you this Wednesday, and also next, which would be very enjoyable for me but, unfortunately, impossible. So grandmother waited for the third Wednesday, but a little girl, a *pipiedda*, always arrived with the letter that put off the visit again, and then there was nothing.

My great-grandfather and her sisters loved her just the same, though she was almost an old maid, but not my great-grandmother; she always treated her as if she were not her own flesh and blood and said that she knew why.

On Sunday, when the girls went to Mass or to parade along the main street with their young men, grandmother gathered her hair into a bun—it was still thick and black when I was a child and she already old, imagine what it was like then—and went to church to ask God why, why he was so unjust as to deny her the knowledge of love, which is the most beautiful thing, the only thing that makes life worth living, a life in which you get up at four in the morning to do the household chores and then you go to the fields and then to the school for boring embroidery and then to get drinking water from the fountain with the pitcher on your head, and then you're up one whole night out of ten to make the bread and then you draw the water from the well and then you have to feed the chickens. So if God didn't want her to know love he might as well kill her, any way he wanted. In confession the priest told her that such thoughts were a serious sin and that there are many other things in the world, but grandmother didn't care at all about other things.

One day my great-grandmother waited for her in the courtyard with the whip, made of ox sinew, and began to hit her until even her head was bleeding and she had a high fever. She had discovered from rumors in the town that the suitors stopped coming because grandmother wrote them passionate love poems that alluded to obscene things and that her daughter was disgracing not only herself but her whole family. And she went on hitting her, hitting her and yelling "*Dimonia! dimonia!*" and cursing the day they had sent her to elementary school, and she had learned to write.

3.

In May of 1943 my grandfather arrived in the town; he was over forty and was an employee of the salt works in Cagliari. He had had a beautiful house on Via Giuseppe Manno, just beside the church of San Giorgio and Santa Caterina, a house with a view over the rooftops to the harbor and the sea. After the bombing of May 13th, nothing was left of this house and the church and many other things, except a hole and a pile of rubble. Grandmother's family welcomed this respectable gentleman, who had not been called up to fight because of his age, who was a very recent widower, an evacuee with only a borrowed suitcase and a few things pulled from the ruins. They took him in for nothing. By June he had asked for grandmother's hand, and married her. She wept almost every day in the month before the marriage. She knelt at my great-grandfather's feet and begged him to say no, to pretend that she was promised to someone away in the war. Otherwise, if they didn't want her in the house anymore, she would go to Cagliari, she would look for a job. "*De Casteddu bèninti innòi, filla mia, e tui bòli si andai ingúni! Non c'esti prus núdda in sa cittàdi*"—"They're coming here from Cagliari, child, and you want to go there! There's nothing left in the city."

"*Macca esti*," my great-grandmother shouted. "*Macca

schetta! In sa cittadi a fai sa baldracca bòliri andai, chi scetti kussu pori fai, chi non sciri fai nudda cummenti si spettada, chi teniri sa conca prena de bentu, de kandu fiada pitíca!"— "She's crazy. Completely crazy! She wants to go to the city to be a whore, that's all she can do, because she doesn't do anything the way it should be done, she's had a head full of air ever since she was a child!"

It would have been simple to invent a fiancé at the front—the Alps, Libya, Albania, the Aegean—or at sea with the Royal Navy. It would have been nothing, but my great-grandparents wouldn't hear of it. So she told him that she didn't love him and could never be a true wife. Grandfather told her not to worry. He didn't love her, either. Assuming that they both knew what they were talking about. As for being a true wife, he understood very well. He would continue to go to the brothel at the port, as he had done since he was a boy, and had never got a disease.

But they did not return to Cagliari until 1945. So my grandparents slept like brother and sister in the guest room: with the big, high iron bedstead inlaid with mother-of-pearl, the painting of the Madonna and Child, the clock under the bell jar, the washstand with pitcher and basin, the mirror with a painted flower, and the porcelain chamber pot under the bed. Those things grandmother brought to Via Giuseppe Manno, when the house in the village was sold; she wanted the room to be exactly the same as the one she had slept in for the first year of her marriage. But in the house in the village the bedrooms got light and air only from the *lolla*, the loggia; here in Via Manno, instead, there is light from the south and from the sea, which invades fiercely until sunset, and makes everything sparkle. And I've always loved this room; when I was a child grandmother let me come in only if I had been good and never more than once a day.

During her first year of marriage grandmother had malaria. The fever rose as high as a hundred and five, and grandfather nursed her, sitting for hours to make sure that the cloth on her forehead stayed cool; her forehead was so hot that the cloth had to be soaked in icy water, and he came and went and you could hear the pulley of the well squeaking day and night.

On one of those days, September 8th, they heard on the radio the news that Italy had asked for an armistice and the war was over. According to grandfather, however, it wasn't over at all, and they had only to hope that the commanding officer, General Basso, would let the Germans leave Sardinia without vain heroics. Basso must have thought like grandfather, because the thirty thousand men of General Lungerhausen's Panzer division left quietly, without slaughtering anyone, and Basso was arrested and put on trial for that, but the Sardinians were saved. Not as on the mainland. And grandfather and the general were right, because then you had only to listen to Radio London, which reported Badoglio's repeated protests against the slaughter of the soldiers and officers who were taken prisoner by the Germans on the Italian front. When grandmother was better they told her that, if not for her husband, the fever would have consumed her, and that there had been the armistice and the change of alliances, and she, with a spitefulness for which she never forgave herself, shrugged her shoulders as if to say, "What do I care."

*

In the high bed at night grandmother curled up as far as possible from him, so that she often fell on the floor, and when, on moonlit nights, the light came through the slats of the doors that opened onto the *lolla* and illuminated her husband's back, she was almost frightened of him, of this alien stranger—she didn't even know if he was handsome or not, since she didn't look at him and he didn't look at her. If grandfather was sleeping soundly, she peed in the chamber pot under the bed; otherwise, it was enough for him to make the slightest movement and she would put on her shawl and leave the room and cross the courtyard to the toilet next to the well. For that matter, grandfather never tried to approach her; he lay stiffly on the other side, though he was a large man, and he, too, often fell off, and they were both always covered with bruises. Alone—that is, in the bedroom—they never spoke. Grandmother said her prayers at night, grandfather didn't, because he was an atheist and a Communist. And then one of them said, "Good night," and the other, "Good night to you, too."

In the morning my great-grandmother wanted her daughter to prepare coffee for grandfather. The coffee of that time was a mixture of chickpeas and orzo toasted in the hearth with a special utensil and then ground. "Bring your husband his coffee," and so grandmother carried the gilt-edged violet cup on the glass tray with floral designs, placed it at the foot of the bed, and immediately ran away, as if she had left a bowl for a mad dog, and she never forgave herself for this, either.

Grandfather helped with the work in the fields and he held up well, even though he was from the city and had spent his life studying and working in an office. He often did his wife's share, too; she now had kidney stones more and more frequently, and he found it shocking that a woman should have to do such heavy work on the land, or carry water from the fountain in a pitcher on her head, and yet, out of respect for the family that was his host, he spoke of these things generally, referring to Sardinian society of the interior. Cagliari was different; there people didn't take offense at a little nothing and didn't find evil everywhere, relentlessly. Maybe it was the sea air that made them freer, at least in certain respects, though not politically, because the Cagliaritani were bourgeois who had never felt like fighting for anything.

Apart from grandmother, who couldn't care less about the world, they listened to Radio London. In the spring of 1944 they learned that in northern Italy six million workers had gone on strike; that in Rome thirty-two Germans had been killed and, in reprisal, the Nazis had rounded up and shot three hundred and twenty Italians; that the Eighth Army was ready for a new offensive; that in the early hours of June 6th the Allies had landed in Normandy.

4.

In November Radio London announced that military operations on the Italian front would be suspended and recommended that the partisans of northern Italy stall for time and use their energies only for sabotage actions.

Grandfather said that the war would continue and he could not be a guest forever, and so they came to Cagliari.

They went to live in Via Sulis, in a furnished room that looked onto a light well and had a bath and kitchen shared with other families. Although she never asked, it was from the neighbors that grandmother learned about grandfather's family, destroyed on May 13, 1943.

Except for him, they were all at home, that terrible afternoon, for his birthday. His wife, a cold, rather plain woman—*leggixedda*—who wasn't friendly with anyone, had that very day, in wartime, made a cake and gathered the family. Who knows when she had bought the ingredients, *a martinicca*, on the black market, gram by gram of sugar, poor woman, poor all of them. No one knows how it happened, but when the alarm sounded they didn't leave the house and hurry to the shelter under the Public Gardens; the most ridiculous reason, but in essence the only one possible, is that the cake was half baked, or was rising, and they didn't want to lose it, that marvelous cake in a dead city. Luckily they didn't have children, the neighbor women said—a wife, a mother, sisters, brothers-in-law, nephews and nieces can be forgotten, and grandfather had forgotten quickly, and it was obvious why, you had only to see how pretty the second wife was. He was a lighthearted man, full-blooded, a womanizer; the Fascists had made him drink castor oil as a boy, to put him in his place, and he had laughed about it later and made jokes, and it seemed that he could survive anything. A good eater, a good drinker, a good client of the brothels, and his wife knew it, poor woman, and surely she had suffered from it, she who was shocked by everything and never let her husband see her naked, though she couldn't have been much to see and you had to wonder what those two did together.

Grandmother, on the other hand, was a womanly woman, as he had certainly always desired, with those big firm breasts and that mass of black hair and those big eyes, and then she was affectionate, and what passion there must be between husband and wife if it had been love at first sight and they married in a month. A pity about those terrible kidney stones, poor thing, they were very fond of her and let her come into the kitchen even at odd hours— whenever she felt well, it didn't matter if maybe they had already cleaned up and put everything away.

Grandmother was a friend of the neighbors of Via Sulis for all her life and theirs. They never had sharp words, in fact they didn't really talk much, but they kept each other company, day after day, come what might. In Via Sulis if they were in the kitchen washing the dishes, one soaped, another rinsed, yet another dried the dishes, and if grand-

mother was ill they did hers, too, *mischinedda*, poor creature. And it was with the neighbors and their husbands
that grandmother followed the last phases of the war. In
the cold kitchen of Via Sulis, with two or three pairs of
darned socks on their feet and their hands under their
armpits, they listened to Radio London.

The husbands, all Communists, cheered for the
Russians, who on January 17, 1945, occupied Warsaw, and
on the twenty-eighth were a hundred and fifty kilometers
from Berlin; in early March the Allies occupied Cologne,
and now, said Churchill, their advance and the German
retreat was a small matter. At the end of March, Patton
and Montgomery crossed the Rhine, pursuing the
Germans in defeat.

The day of grandfather's birthday, May 13th, the war
was over and everyone was happy, but to grandmother
those advances and retreats and victories and defeats
meant nothing. In the city there was no water, sewers, elec-
tric light; there wasn't even food except for American
soup, and the price of everything went up by three hundred per cent, but the neighbors when they washed the
dishes laughed at some *sciollorio*, any silly thing, and even
when they went to Mass, at Sant'Antonio, or Santa Rosalia,
or at the Capuchins, they were always laughing, in the
street, three in front and three behind, in their turned
dresses. And grandmother didn't say much, but she was
always there, too, and the days flowed by and she liked the
way in Cagliari the neighbors weren't so melodramatic as
in the country, and if something went wrong they said,
"*Ma bbai!*" If for example a plate fell on the floor and
broke, even though they were poor they shrugged and

picked up the pieces. Basically they were content to be poor, better than having money like so many in Cagliari who had made fortunes off the misery of others, on the black market or stealing amid the ruins before the unfortunate people came in search of their things. And then they were alive *mi naras nudda!*—you're telling me. Grandmother thought it was because of the sea and the blue sky, and the immensity you saw from the Bastioni—the ramparts—in the mistral: it was all so infinite that you couldn't pause on your own little life.

But she didn't express these rather poetic ideas, because she was terrified that these people, too, would discover that she was mad. She wrote everything down in her black notebook with the red border and then she hid it in the drawer of secret things, with the money envelopes marked "Food," "Medicine," "Rent."

5.

One evening, grandfather, before sitting down in the dilapidated armchair near the window on the light well, went and got his pipe from his evacuee's suitcase, took out of his pocket a pouch of tobacco he had just bought, and began to smoke, for the first time since that May of 1943. Grandmother brought over her chair and sat looking at him.

"That's how you smoke a pipe. I've never seen anyone smoke a pipe."

And they sat in silence the whole time. When grandfather finished she said to him, "You shouldn't spend any more money on the women in the brothel. You should spend that money to buy tobacco, and relax and have your smoke. Explain to me what you do with those women and I'll do the same."

6.

In the days of Via Sulis her kidney stones were frightening, and every day it seemed as if she would die. Surely that was the reason she couldn't have children, even now, when they had a bit more money, and they'd take the short walk to Via Manno to see the devastated place where they hoped to rebuild their house, which they were steadily saving for. They especially liked to look at the pit when grandmother got pregnant, except that in the end all the stones she had inside her always turned the joy into sorrow, and blood everywhere.

Until 1947 people were starving, and grandmother remembered how happy she was when she went to her village and came back all loaded down. She'd run up the stairs and into the kitchen, which always smelled of cabbage because not much air came in from the light well, and place on the marble tabletop two loaves of *civraxiu* and fresh pasta and cheese and eggs and a chicken for broth. Those good smells covered up the odor of cabbage and the neighbors welcomed her warmly and told her she was so pretty because she was good.

In those days she was happy, even if she didn't have love, happy with the things of the world even if grandfather never touched her except when she performed the brothel services; and in bed they continued to sleep on opposite sides, taking care not to touch, and saying, "Good night."

"Good night to you, too."

The best moments were when, in bed after her services, grandfather lighted his pipe and it was clear from his expression that he felt good. Grandmother would look at him from her side and if she smiled at him he said, "Does this amuse you?" But it wasn't as if he ever added anything else, or drew her to him; he kept her distant. And grandmother always thought how strange love is, if it doesn't want to come it won't, with bed or even with kindness and good deeds, and it was strange that here was the most important thing, and there was no way to make it happen, by any means.

7

In 1950 the doctors prescribed thermal treatments for her. They instructed her to go to the mainland, to a well-known spa, where many people had been cured. So grandmother again put on her gray sack overcoat with three buttons, the one from her wedding, which I've seen in the few photographs of those years, embroidered two blouses, put everything in grandfather's evacuee's suitcase, and left by ship for Civitavecchia.

The spa was in a place that was not at all beautiful; there was no sun, and from the bus that went from the station to the hotel all she could see was earth-colored hills with a few tufts of tall grass around spectral trees. Besides, everyone on the bus seemed ill and pale. When the chestnut allées and the hotels began to appear, she asked the driver to let her know which was the stop for her hotel. She stood for a while at the entrance wondering whether to run away or not: it was all so alien and grim, under that cloudy sky, that she thought she was already in the Hereafter, because this could only be death. The hotel was very elegant, with crystal-teardrop chandeliers that were all lighted, even though it was early afternoon. In her room she immediately noticed a desk under the window, and maybe it was only because of that that she didn't flee to the station and then to the ship and home again, though grandfather would have been very angry if she had, and with reason. She had never had a desk, nor had she ever been able to sit at a table to write, because she always wrote secretly, with the notebook on her lap, and she hid it whenever she heard someone coming. On the desk there was a leather folder with sheets of letterhead, an inkwell, a pen and nib, and blotting paper. So the first thing grandmother did, even before taking off her coat, was to get her notebook out of the suitcase and place it ceremoniously on the desk, in the leather folder; then she locked the door, out of fear that someone might enter and see what was written in the notebook; and finally she sat down on the big double bed and waited for dinnertime. The dining room was filled with square tables with white linen tablecloths and white porcelain plates and sparkling glasses and silverware and, in the middle, a vase of flowers, and over each hung a beautiful glowing crystal chandelier. Some of the tables were already occupied by people who seemed to her like souls from Purgatory, because of their melancholy pallor and the indistinct, low murmur of their voices, but there were still many places free. Grandmother chose an empty table and on the three other chairs placed her purse, her coat, and her wool jacket, and when someone passed by she looked down, hoping that the person wouldn't sit next to her. She had no wish to eat, or to have the treatments, because she was sure she wouldn't get better and would never have children. Normal women had children, cheerful women without ugly thoughts, like the neighbors of Via Sulis. Children, as soon as they realized they were in the belly of a madwoman, fled, as all those suitors had.

A man with a suitcase entered the dining room; he must have just arrived and not yet been to his own room. He carried a crutch, but he walked quickly and easily. That man attracted grandmother, unlike any of the suitors to whom she had written passionate poems and waited for Wednesday after Wednesday. She was sure, then, that she wasn't in the Hereafter, with the other souls of Purgatory, because such a thing doesn't happen in the Hereafter.

The Veteran had a modest suitcase, but he was dressed with great refinement, and although he had a wooden leg and a crutch he was a handsome man. In her room after dinner, grandmother sat down at the desk right away to describe him in detail, so that, if she never saw him again in the hotel, there was no danger of forgetting him. He was tall, with dark, deep eyes, smooth skin, a slender neck; he had strong, long arms and large, innocent hands, like a child's; he had a full mouth, prominent in spite of the short, slightly curling beard, and a gently curved nose.

In the following days she looked at him from her table or on the veranda, where he went to smoke unfiltered Nationals or read, and she did her boring cross-stitch embroidery on napkins. She always arranged her chair a little behind him, in order not to be seen as she gazed, spellbound, at the line of his forehead, the thin nose, the defenseless throat, the curly hair with its first white threads, the poignant thinness of the chest in the starched pure-white shirt with the sleeves rolled up, the strong arms and the good hands, the leg rigid in the trousers, the old but perfectly polished shoes—all to make you weep for the dignity of that body, injured but still inexplicably strong and handsome.

Then came days of sun and everything seemed different, the gilded chestnuts, the blue sky, and the veranda, where the Veteran went to smoke or read and grandmother pretended to embroider, was flooded with light.

He rose and went to look at the hills beyond the windows and stood there thoughtfully, and when he turned to go and sit down again he looked at her and smiled a melting smile that almost made my grandmother ill she liked it so much, and that emotion filled her day.

One evening as the Veteran passed grandmother's table he seemed uncertain where to sit, so she took away her coat and purse to make room for him next to her. He sat down and, smiling, they looked into each other's eyes, and that evening they ate and drank nothing. The Veteran suffered from the same illness, and his kidneys, too, were full of stones. He had fought the whole war. As a boy he was always reading novels by Salgari and had volunteered for the Navy; he loved the sea and literature, especially poetry, and this had sustained him in the most difficult moments. When the war was over he got his degree and had recently moved from Genoa to Milan, where he taught Italian, making every effort not to bore the students. He lived on the mezzanine floor of a *casa di ringhiera*, where the apartments opened onto a balcony overlooking a courtyard, in two white rooms that contained nothing of the past. He had been married since 1939 and had a daughter in the first year of elementary school; she was drawing the letters of the alphabet and Greek key patterns, which was the custom then, making designs like the ones embroidered by grandmother on the napkins, but in a notebook with graph paper, and these Greek key patterns framed the pages. His daughter loved school, the smell of books and stationery. She loved rain and had a fondness for umbrellas, and they had bought her one that was striped like a beach umbrella; in that season it was always raining in Milan, but the child would wait for him in any type of weather, sitting on the steps or skipping in the big inner courtyard, which the less elegant apartments faced. And then in Milan there was the fog, which grandmother had no idea about: from the description she imagined a situation like the Hereafter. Grandmother on the other hand had no children. Certainly because of those stones in her kidneys. She, too, had loved school, but her parents had taken her out in fourth grade. The teacher had come to their house to ask them to send her to high school, or at least have her enroll at a trade school, because she wrote well. Her parents were afraid that they would in some way be obligated to let her continue her studies, and they had kept her home and told the teacher that he didn't understand their problems and not to come back. But by then she had learned to read and write and had been secretly writing all her life now. Poems. Maybe thoughts. Things that happened to her, but partly invented. No one was to know, because they might think she was crazy. She was confiding in him because she trusted him, even though she had known him scarcely an hour. The Veteran was keenly interested and made her promise solemnly not to be embarrassed and to let him read the poems, if she had them with her, or recite them, because to him the others seemed mad, not her. He, too, had a passion: playing the piano. He had loved it since he was a child—it was a passion that came from his mother—and whenever he was home on leave he played for hours and hours. His highest accomplishment was the Chopin Nocturnes; but when he returned from the war the piano wasn't there, and he hadn't had the heart to ask his wife what had happened to it. Now he had bought another one and his fingers were starting to remember.

Here at the baths he missed the piano, but that was before he began talking to grandmother, because talking to grandmother and watching her laugh or even feel sad, and seeing how her hair came loose when she gestured, or admiring the skin of her slender wrists and the contrast with her chapped hands—that was like playing the piano.

From that day grandmother and the Veteran were inseparable, parting only reluctantly, when they went to the bathroom. They didn't care about the gossip, he because he was from the North, and grandmother, though she was Sardinian, hardly.

In the morning they met in the breakfast room: the one who got there first ate slowly, to give the other time to arrive. Every day grandmother was afraid that the Veteran might leave without telling her, or that he was tired of her company, or maybe would change tables and pass her by with a cold nod of greeting, like all those men of the Wednesdays so many years before. But he always chose the same table, and if it was she who arrived later she knew that he was waiting for her, since he was having a cup of coffee, and nothing else, and she would find him sitting there with the now empty cup in front of him. The Veteran would instantly grab his crutch and stand up as if to salute his Captain, bow his head slightly, and say, "Good morning Princess," and my grandmother would laugh, moved and happy.

"Princess of what?"

Then he invited her to come with him to buy the newspaper, which he read every day, like grandfather, except that grandfather read it to himself, in silence, while the Veteran sat on a bench with her beside him and read articles aloud to her and asked her opinion and it didn't matter that he had a degree and grandmother had only gone to fourth grade: it was clear that he gave great consideration to her ideas. For example, he asked her about the Fund for the South, what did the Sardinians say about it? And about the Korean War, what did grandmother think? And what about what was happening in China? Grandmother would have him explain the matter carefully and then she expressed her opinion, and she couldn't imagine giving up the news of the day, her head touching the Veteran's during the reading, so close that in an instant they might have kissed.

Then he said, "And what streets shall we take back to the hotel today? Suggest a route you'd like to follow."

So they always went a different way, and when the Veteran saw that grandmother had suddenly stopped in the middle of the street, distracted, her attention caught by the façade of a hotel or the leaves of a tree, or who knows what, as was her habit all the way into old age, he placed a hand on her back and, pressing lightly, guided her to the side of the street. "A princess. You act like a princess. You don't worry about the world around you; it's the world that should worry about you. Your job is merely to exist. Isn't that true?"

And grandmother was amused by this fantasy—the future princess of Via Manno and now of Via Sulis and before that of Campidano.

Without making a precise appointment they arrived at breakfast earlier and earlier, and so they had more time for reading the newspaper side by side on the bench, and for the walk, where it always turned out that the Veteran had to put his hand on her back and make her change direction.

One day the Veteran asked grandmother if he could see her whole arm, and when she pulled up the sleeve of her blouse he ran his index finger intently over the veins on the surface of the skin.

"Beauty," he said, and then, "You are a true beauty. But why all these cuts?"

Grandmother answered that it was from working in the fields.

"But they seem to have been made with the blade of a knife."

"We cut so many things. It's like that in farm work."

"Then why your arms and not your hands? Those are clean cuts—they look intentional."

She didn't answer and he took her hand and kissed it and with his finger touched the lines of her face. "Beauty," he repeated, "beauty."

Then she touched him as well, that man she had observed for days from her chair on the veranda, as delicately as she would have touched the sculpture of a great artist: the hair, the soft skin of the neck, the fabric of his shirt, his strong arms and nice childlike hands, the wooden leg and the foot inside the freshly polished shoe.

The Veteran's daughter wasn't his. In 1944 he was a prisoner of the Germans, who were retreating eastward. His daughter was in fact the daughter of a partisan, whom his wife had fought alongside, and who had been killed during an action. The Veteran loved his daughter and had no wish to know more.

He had left in 1940, embarking on the cruiser Trieste, had been shipwrecked two or three times, had been captured in 1943, off Marseilles, interned in the concentration camp at Hinzert until 1944, and had lost his leg during the retreat of the winter of '44-'45: the Allies had arrived when he was still able to drag himself along, and an American doctor had amputated the leg to save his life.

They were sitting on a bench and grandmother took his head in her hands and placed it on her heart, which was beating wildly, and unbuttoned the top buttons of her blouse. He caressed her breast with his smiling lips. "Shall we kiss our smiles?" grandmother asked, and so they kissed, an endless, liquid kiss, and the Veteran told her that in the fifth Canto of the Inferno Dante had had this very idea of the smiles that kiss, for Paolo and Francesca, two who loved each other and could not.

Grandmother's house, like the Veteran's piano, was to be reborn from the ruins: a building was planned for the large hole left by the church of San Giorgio and Santa Caterina and grandfather's old house. She was sure that her house would be beautiful, full of light, with a view of the ships from the rooms and the orange and purple sunsets and the swallows that would leave for Africa, and on the floor below a room for parties, the winter garden, and a red runner on the stairs, and a gurgling fountain on the terrace. Via Manno was beautiful, the most beautiful street in Cagliari. On Sundays grandfather brought her pastries from Tramer and on other days when he wanted to give her pleasure he bought octopus at the market of Santa Chiara, which she boiled with oil and salt and parsley. The Veteran's wife, on the other hand, now made cutlets and risotto, but the best things still were Genoese: pesto with *trenette*, stuffed veal breast, and Easter cake. The Veteran's house in Genoa was near the Gaslini hospital and had a garden with fig trees, hortensia, violets, and a chicken coop; he had always lived there. Now he had sold it to some nice people who, whenever he came as a guest, gave him fresh eggs and, in summer, tomatoes and basil to take back to Milan. It was a damp old house, but the garden was lovely, inundated by the plants. The only valuable thing in the house had been the piano, from his mother. She was from a very wealthy family, but had fallen in love with his father, a *camallo*, a dock worker, and so the family had turned her out, and the only thing they let her have, and this was long afterward, was her piano. When he was a child, his mother, especially in the summer, after dinner—because in Genoa it was the custom to eat early and then go out—would take him to see his grandparents' villa from the outside: the high wall all along the street up to the big gate and the gatehouse next to it, and the allée of palm trees and agave, and the lawn, with flowers in geometric patterns, that rose up and up to the grand milk-white three-story structure, which had terraces with plaster balustrades, and ice-colored stuccowork around the rows of windows, many of them illuminated, and, at the top, four towers.

But his mother told him that none of that mattered, she had the love of her husband, and the love of her son, her *figeto*, and she hugged him tight and on summer nights in Genoa there were so many fireflies that he remembered his mother just like that.

She had died when the Veteran was not yet ten, and his father had never remarried; he went to the women in the brothel on Via Pre, and that had seemed sufficient until he died, in the Allied bombing, while he was still working at the port.

Maybe the Veteran's daughter wasn't the daughter of a partisan. Maybe she was the daughter of a German and his wife didn't want to tell him, so that he wouldn't hate her, as the daughter of a Nazi. Maybe she had had to defend herself. Maybe a German soldier had helped her. She worked in a factory, and certainly in March of 1943 had gone on strike for bread, peace, and freedom. She had never forgiven him the military uniform, even though everyone knew that the Royal Navy was loyal to the king and barely tolerated Fascism—or the Germans, who were mountain people—because its allies were supposed to be the English, and those who enlisted were not caught up in the delirium of the time; they were serious, modest people, with a great sense of sacrifice and honor.

His daughter already had a Milanese accent, a doll she played mother with, a miniature kitchen and a set of china, and notebooks with the first letters of the alphabet and the Greek key design. She liked it when you were on the train to Genoa and the sea appeared suddenly at the end of a tunnel, and she had cried when, a year ago, they moved to Milan: she would sit on the balcony and call to the passersby, "Genoa! Give me back my Genoa! I want my Genoa!" If she was the daughter of a German he was a good German.

Grandmother also had the idea, although she didn't understand politics, that the German invaders of Italy couldn't possibly all have been bad people. And then what about the Americans, who had destroyed Cagliari, had really almost razed it to the ground? Her husband, who did understand politics and read the newspaper every day and was a very intelligent Communist, and had organized the workers' strike at the salt works, always said there was no strategic reason to damage the city so severely, and yet the pilots of the B17s, the flying fortresses, couldn't all have been evil, right? There must have been some good people among them, too.

And now the house on Via Manno and the piano would fill the hole, and the Veteran embraced grandmother and whispered in her ear the sounds of the bass, the trumpet, the violin, the flute. He knew how to do the whole orchestra. It might seem crazy, but during the long marches in the snow, or in the concentration camp when he had to fight dogs for food to amuse the Germans, poetry and those sounds in his mind had sustained him.

He also told her, still whispering in her ear, that some scholars maintain that Paolo and Francesca were murdered as soon as they were discovered, while other Dantists think that they had the pleasure of one another for a while, before they died. "And that day we read no farther" has to be interpreted. He said also that if grandmother wasn't too afraid of Hell they could love each other in that same way. And grandmother had no fear of Hell, imagine. If God was truly God, and knew how much she had longed for love, how much she had prayed at least to know what it was, how could he now send her to Hell.

And then what a Hell if, even as an old woman, when she thought back to it she smiled at the image of herself and the Veteran and that kiss. And if she was sad she cheered herself with the photograph that she had fixed in her mind.

8.

My grandmother was over sixty when I was born. I remember that as a child I thought she was beautiful, and I'd watch, enthralled, when she combed her hair and made her old-fashioned *crocchia*, parting the hair, which never turned white, or thin, then braiding it and coiling the braids into two chignons. I felt proud when she picked me up at school, with her youthful smile, amid the mothers and fathers of the others; mine, being musicians, were always traveling around the world. My grandmother was all for me, at least as much as my father was all for music and my mother all for my father.

Papa never had a girlfriend, and grandmother suffered and felt guilty thinking that she might have transmitted to her son the mysterious illness that caused love to flee. At that time there were clubs where boys and girls went dancing and embarked on love affairs along with Beatles songs, but not my father. Sometimes he rehearsed pieces with girls at the Conservatory, singers, violinists, flutists—they all wanted him to accompany them on the piano at their exams, since he was the best, but when the exam was over so was everything else.

Then one day grandmother went to the door and there was mamma, with her flute over her shoulder, all out of breath, because here in Via Manno there's no elevator. She had a shy but confident look, just as my mother has now, and she was pretty, simple, fresh, and, panting because of the steep stairs, she laughed for no reason, joyously, the way girls laugh, and grandmother called papa, who was shut in his room playing, and cried, "She's here. The person you were expecting is here!"

Mamma can never forget that day: they had to practice a piece for piano and flute and none of the practice rooms at the Conservatory were free, so my father told her to come to Via Manno. Everything seemed perfect to her, grandmother, grandfather, the house. She lived on the outskirts, in an ugly neighborhood of gray barracks-like apartments, with her widowed mother, my grandmother Lia, who was severe and rigid and obsessed with order and hygiene, who waxed the floors and made you put on felt slippers, and always wore black, and whom mamma had to telephone constantly to say where she was, but she never complained. The only happy thing in mamma's life was music, which Signora Lia couldn't bear: she closed all the doors in order not to hear her daughter practice.

Mamma had loved my father silently for a long time; she liked everything about him, even the fact that he was utterly in another world, and always had his sweaters on backward and never remembered what season it was and wore summer shirts until he caught bronchitis, and everyone said he was crazy. So although he was very handsome, girls didn't want to go with him for all those reasons, and especially because that kind of craziness wasn't fashionable then, and, after all, neither was classical music, in which he was a genius. Mamma, however, would have sold her soul for him.

At first she kept herself free on purpose and didn't even look for a job, because that was the only way to stay with papa: turning the pages of the few scores he didn't know by heart, sitting on the stool next to him, touring all over the world. Even if it was impossible for her to go with him, for example when I was born, he went. The day of my birth he was in New York, for Ravel's Concerto in G. My grandparents didn't telephone, because they didn't want to excite him, fearful that he might play badly because of me. So as soon as I grew a little, mamma bought a duplicate playpen, duplicate baby walker, duplicate high chair, duplicate warming dish, and brought everything here to Via Manno, so that she could pack a bag of baby clothes, hand me over to grandmother, and immediately get the plane to join papa.

But they never left me with my maternal grandmother, Signora Lia; if they tried, I'd cry desperately. Whatever I did, a drawing, for example, or maybe if I sang her a song with words I had made up, that other grandmother darkened and said there are more important things, one has to think of the important things, and I got the idea that she hated my parents' music, hated the storybooks that I always had with me. To please her I tried to understand what might gratify her, but she didn't seem to like anything. Mamma told me that Signora Lia was like that because her husband had died, even before mamma was born, and because she had quarreled with her wealthy family and had left Gavoi, her town, which to her was ugly.

I don't remember my grandfather; he died when I was too young, on May 10, 1978, the day Law 180 was passed, the law that closed down the insane asylums. My father always told me that he was an exceptional man and everyone respected him tremendously and grandmother's relatives loved him dearly because he had saved her from so many things it was better to forget about it, except that I was to be careful with grandmother, I mustn't upset her, or agitate her too much. There was always a veil of mystery over her, perhaps of pity.

Only as an adult did I learn that before meeting grandfather, in May of 1943, she had thrown herself down the well, and her sisters, hearing the thud, had rushed into the courtyard and called the neighbors, and they had miraculously managed to pull her out, all holding onto the rope together; and that once she had disfigured herself by cutting her hair so she looked like a mangy dog; and she was always cutting the veins in her arms. I knew a different grandmother, who would laugh at a trifle, and my father said the same, that in his life, too, she was peaceful, except for once, and maybe those other things were only stories. But I know they're true. Besides, grandmother always said that her life was divided into two parts: before and after the treatment at the thermal baths, as if the water that had enabled her to get rid of the stones had been miraculous in all senses.

9.

Nine months after she returned from the baths my father was born, in 1951, and when he was just seven grandmother went to work as a maid for two women, Donna Doloretta and Donna Fanní, in Viale Luigi Merello, in secret from grandfather and everyone else, because she intended to have her son take piano lessons. The ladies felt sorry for her: to them this business of the music seemed crazy, *"Narami tui chi no è macca una chi podia biviri beni e faidi sa zeracca poita su fillu depidi sonai su piano"*—"You tell me she isn't mad—a woman who could live comfortably and goes to work as a maid because her son has to play the piano." But they liked her so much that they gave her special hours: she came to work after taking papa to school, the Sebastian Satta, and left early to pick him up and do the shopping, and if the offices and schools were on vacation she was, too. Grandfather must have wondered why she always did her household chores in the afternoon, when she had all the morning free, but he never asked her and never reproached her if he found things untidy or lunch wasn't ready. Maybe he thought that his wife listened to records in the morning, now that they were doing better economically and she had developed this passion for music, Chopin, Debussy, Beethoven, and listened to operas, weeping at "Madame Butterfly"

and "La Traviata"; or he supposed that she took the tram
to the Poetto beach to see the sea, or maybe to have coffee
with her friends Donna Doloretta and Donna Fanní.
Whereas grandmother, having taken papa to Via Angioy,
swiftly ascended Via Don Bosco to Viale Merello, where
all the villas had palm trees and terraces with plaster
balustrades, and gardens with fish ponds and fountains
with putti. The ladies did expect her for coffee and they
served it on a silver tray, before she started work, because
grandmother was a real lady. They talked about the men in
their lives: Donna Fanní's fiancé had died at Vittorio
Veneto fighting in the Sassari Brigade, and she was always
sad on October 24th, when the victory was celebrated.
Grandmother talked, too, not, of course, about the
Veteran or the madness or the brothel, but about the suitors who fled, yes, and about grandfather, who had loved
her right away and married her, and the ladies looked at
each other in embarrassment, as if to say it was glaringly
obvious that he had married her to repay his debt to the
family, but they were silent. Maybe they thought that she
was a little strange and wasn't aware of things, certainly
"*su macchiòri de sa musica e de su piano*," her madness for
music and the piano, must have been pure madness to
them, since they had a piano and never touched it; they
placed doilies on it with vases of flowers and various other
objects, while grandmother practically caressed it before
she dusted and polished it, using her breath and a cloth
she had bought just for that purpose. One day the ladies
made her a proposal: they were accustomed to having servants, but they had no money and could no longer continue to pay grandmother; however, a price could be set
for the piano, and grandmother would pay for it daily, by

doing the housework, and to her husband she would say that it was a gift from them, her friends. They also added the built-in lamp that illuminated the keyboard, but grandmother had to sell that right away, to pay for the transport from Viale Merello to Via Manno and the tuning. The day the piano traveled to Via Manno she felt such a rush of happiness that she ran from Viale Merello to Via Manno ahead of the truck, reciting in her mind the first lines of a poem that the Veteran had written for her, faster and faster, all in one breath without periods or commas: *If you left a faint mark on life that moves like a snake If you left a faint mark on life that moves like a snake If you left a faint mark on life that moves like a snake.* They put the piano in the big, light-filled room overlooking the port. And papa was good.

He really is. At times the newspapers talk about him, saying he's the only Sardinian who has ever really been successful in the music world, and they roll out the red carpet for him in the concert halls of Paris, London, New York. Grandfather had an album covered in bottle-green leather just for the photographs and newspaper clippings about his son's concerts.

My father always talked to me about grandfather in particular.

He loved his mother, but she was alien to him, and when she asked him a question about how things were going he answered, "Normal, ma. Everything's normal." Then grandmother said that things couldn't be normal, they had of necessity to be one way rather than another, and it was evident that she got upset and jealous when the three of them were sitting at the table and, in grandfather's presence, the things of the world acquired that "way" which she had spoken of. Now that his mother is dead papa can't forgive himself, but nothing ever came to mind. She went to a concert of his only once, when he was a boy, but she fled, overcome by emotion. Grandfather, who was always protecting her—although not even he ever knew what to say to her and he certainly wasn't affectionate—didn't follow her and stayed to enjoy his son's concert. He had been very happy and couldn't stop praising him.

Papa is glad that for me, on the other hand, it's been easy. Better. Better like that. Besides, grandmother brought me up. I was always in Via Manno more than in my own house, and I never wanted to leave when he and mamma came home. As a child I had terrible tantrums, screaming and crawling under the beds, or I'd lock myself in a room and make them swear to let me stay before I would come out. One day I even hid in a big empty flower vase and stuck some branches in my hair. And then the next day the same thing. I refused to take my dolls and games home. Then, when I was older, books. I said that I had to stay at grandmother's to study because it was especially inconvenient to carry the dictionaries. Or if I invited friends over I preferred grandmother's because there was the terrace. And so on. Maybe I loved her in the right way. With my scenes and tears and yelling and rushes of happiness. When I came back from a trip she was down in the street waiting and I ran to meet her and we hugged each other and wept from emotion as if I had been to war and not off having fun.

Since grandmother never came to papa's concerts, I got on the telephone afterward from the various cities of the world and described everything to her, in great detail, and even did a little of the music for her and told her what the applause had been like and what a sensation the performance had caused. Or, if the concert was nearby, I came to Via Manno right away, and grandmother sat down and listened to me with her eyes closed, and she smiled and beat time with her feet in her slippers.

Signora Lia, however, couldn't stand papa's concerts and said that her son-in-law didn't have a real job, that his success might end at any moment and there he'd be, with mamma and me, a beggar if it weren't for his parents, but only as long as they were alive. She knew what it meant to manage on your own and not ask anyone for help. She, unfortunately, had known real life. My father wasn't bothered by this, or maybe he wasn't aware of the contempt of his mother-in-law, who never paid him a compliment and regularly threw out the newspapers with articles about him or used them to clean the windows or to put under the feet of workers who came to make repairs in the house.

Papa has always had his music, and nothing else in the world matters to him.

10

About the suitors who fled, about the well, about the hair like a mangy dog, about the scars on her arms, and about the brothel—grandmother told the Veteran all of this the first night they spent together at risk of ending up in Hell. And grandmother said that there were only two people she had really talked to in her life: to him and to me. He was the thinnest and the handsomest man she had ever seen, and it was the most intense and prolonged lovemaking. Because the Veteran, before he penetrated her, again and again, slowly undressed her, stopping to caress every part of her body, smiling at her and telling her that she was beautiful. He wanted to take the pins out of her hair himself and, like a child, sink his hands in that black cloud of curls, and unbutton her clothes and gaze at her lying naked on the bed, so he could admire her large firm breasts, her soft white skin, her long legs, and all the while he caressed her and kissed her where she had never been kissed. She could have fainted with pleasure. And then grandmother undressed him, carefully placing the wooden leg at the foot of the bed, and she kissed and caressed his stump for a long time. And for the first time she thanked God in her heart for having brought her into the world, for having pulled her out of the well, for having given her a beautiful bosom and beautiful hair and even, in fact especially, kidney stones.

Afterward he told her that she was very good and that he had never encountered anyone like her in any brothel at any price. Then grandmother proudly listed her services. The prey: the man captures the woman, naked, in a fishing net in which he makes one opening, just so he can penetrate her. She is his fish. He touches her everywhere, but feels only the shapes and not the skin. The slave: she gives him a bath and caresses him with bare breasts, and offers them to him to bite but doesn't dare look at him. The geisha: he simply has her tell him stories that take him away from the problems of daily life; she is completely clothed and they don't necessarily make love. The lunch: she lies down and the man spreads the food out as if on a table that has been set, for example a piece of fruit in her vagina or jam on her breast or ragù or custard, and eats everything. The girl: it's he who gives her a bath in the tub, with lots of bubbles; he washes her all over and in gratitude she will take him in her mouth. The muse: he photographs her in the most indecent poses, with her thighs spread, while she masturbates and squeezes her tits. The dog-woman: she wears only a bra and brings him the newspaper in her mouth, while he pats her sex from behind or her hair or ears and says, "Good dog." The servant: she brings him coffee in bed wearing an outfit that's modest but reveals her breasts almost completely, and she lets him milk them, then she climbs the wardrobe to clean and isn't wearing underpants. The lazybones: she is tied to the bed because she has to be punished with the belt, but grandfather never really hurt her. Grandmother always performed outstandingly and after every service her husband told her how much it would have cost at the brothel. They put that sum away for rebuilding the house on Via Manno, and grandmother insisted that a small amount be used for pipe tobacco. But they continued to sleep on opposite sides of the bed and never spoke about themselves, and maybe that was why grandmother couldn't forget the emotion she felt on those nights with the Veteran, with his arm around her head and his hand sleeping but present, seeming to caress her hair. The Veteran said that in his view her husband was a lucky man, really, and not, as she said, unfortunate, cursed with a poor madwoman; she wasn't mad, she was a creature made at a moment when God simply had no wish for the usual mass-produced women and, being in a poetic vein, had created her. Grandmother laughed heartily and said that he was mad, too, and so wasn't aware of the madness of others.

On one of the following nights the Veteran told grandmother that his father hadn't died during one of the bombings of Genoa but had been tortured by the Gestapo. His body had been thrown into the street outside the Casa dello Studente, disfigured by brutal wounds. But he hadn't told where his daughter-in-law was, or the partisans who had been telegraphing from his house to the Allies. He had insisted on staying in the house so that everything would seem normal to those who were watching them after the tip-off, and so the others had been able to escape into the Apennines. He wanted his son and daughter-in-law to have a family, he had told her as he said goodbye, and then he had sat down to wait for the Gestapo. The Veteran's daughter was born in the mountains. But maybe it wasn't true, he had heard that she was the daughter of a German. He couldn't even imagine his wife in love with someone else, so he felt that the father of his daughter was a monster who perhaps had taken her violently, surely when she had tried to save her father-in-law. And he had never been able to touch that woman again, that was why they hadn't had children. He, too, had become a habitué of the brothels. The Veteran burst into tears and then he was horribly ashamed, because he had been taught as a boy never to show grief. Then grandmother also began to cry, saying that she instead had been taught not to show joy, and maybe that had been right, because the only thing that had gone well for her, marrying grandfather, she was indifferent to, and she never understood why those suitors all fled, but anyway what do we really know about others, what did the Veteran know.

On the subject of not understanding, she had once got up her courage and, with her heart beating so hard she thought it would burst out of her chest, asked grandfather if, now that he knew her better—not that, for heaven's sake, knowing her better was a great thing—but anyway if, having lived with her all this time and having no need to go to the brothel anymore, he loved her. And grandfather had sort of smiled to himself, without looking at her, and then he had given her a pat on the behind and hadn't even dreamed of answering. Another time, during a service that she couldn't tell the Veteran about, grandfather said she had the most beautiful ass he had ever had in his life. And so what can we know, truly, even about those closest to us.

11

In 1963, grandmother went with her husband and papa to visit her sister and brother-in-law who had emigrated to Milan.

The house in the village had been sold to help the sisters, and my grandparents had given up their share, but still the others couldn't make it, three families farming a property of less than twenty hectares. The agrarian reforms had been cautious and the Rebirth Plan was all wrong, as it was based on the chemical and iron and steel industries, and, having been initiated by people from the mainland with public funds, did nothing for us here, grandfather said; rather, the future of Sardinia would have been in manufacturing, which would have made use of the existing resources. For the other two sisters, who lived on the land, it made things easier, in the end, when one had left. Grandmother had suffered a lot and didn't even go to San Gavino to see her youngest sister, her brother-in-law, and their children take the train for Porto Torres. And she had suffered for the house, too. The new owners had replaced the arched front entrance with an iron gate. The wooden pilasters, and the low wall separating her *lolla* from the courtyard, had been knocked down, and the *lolla* closed in by aluminum-frame windows. The low upper floor, which looked out over the roof of the *lolla*, and where the hayloft had been, had become a mansard, like the ones you see in postcards of the Alps. The stalls for the oxen and the woodshed made into a garage for cars. The flower beds reduced to a narrow perimeter along the wall. The well plugged up with cement. The tile roof, above the loft that was now a mansard, replaced by a terrace with a hollow-brick parapet. The multicolored terracotta tiles, which made kaleidoscopic designs on the floor, covered by outdoor tile. And the furniture was too much for the space of the rooms that the sisters now occupied in the houses of their husbands' families, and no one wanted it—so old and cumbersome, from a time best forgotten. Only grandmother had taken the things from the bedroom she had had as a new bride, to re-create it in Via Giuseppe Manno.

By the time they made the trip to Milan she knew that the family had grown prosperous, because her sister wrote to her that *Milàn l'è il gran Milàn*, Milan is the great Milan, and there was work for everyone and on Saturday they shopped at the supermarket and filled carts with perfectly packaged food, and that idea they had always had of economizing, of cutting no more than the exact number of slices of bread, of turning their coats, jackets, suits, of unraveling sweaters to reuse the wool, of resoling their shoes a thousand times—all done with. In Milan they went to the big department stores and got new clothes. What she didn't like was the climate, the smog that blackened the edges of the sleeves and shirt collars and the children's school smocks. She was constantly having to wash everything, but in Milan there was lots of water—they didn't offer it on alternate days, as in Sardinia, and you could let it run and run, without worrying about washing yourself first, then with the waste water washing the clothes, then throwing the dirty water into the toilet. In Milan washing and bathing were fun. And then her sister didn't have much to do after the housework, which was soon done, because the houses were small; millions of inhabitants had to live in that space—it wasn't like Sardinia, with its enormous houses that were of no use to anyone, since they had no conveniences. In short, she had soon finished the housework and then she wandered around the city looking in the stores, and shopping.

My grandparents didn't know what to bring to the wealthy relatives in Milan. After all, they didn't need anything. So grandmother proposed a poetic package, for old times' sake, because it was true that they ate and dressed well, but Sardinian sausage and a nice Pecorino and oil and wine from Marmilla and a side of prosciutto and marinated cardoons and sweaters for the children hand-knitted by grandmother would bring them the fragrance of home.

They set off without letting the relatives know. It would be a surprise. Grandfather got a map of Milan and studied the streets and planned itineraries for seeing the best sights in the city.

They all three got new clothes in order not to make a bad impression. Grandmother bought some Elizabeth Arden cream, because now she was fifty and wanted the Veteran—her heart told her that they would meet—to find her still beautiful. Not that she was very worried by this.

People always said that a man of fifty would never look at a woman the same age, but this reasoning was valid only for the things of the world. Not love. Love doesn't care about age or anything else that isn't love. And it was with that love that the Veteran had loved her. Who could say if he would recognize her right away. What sort of expression he would have. They would not embrace in the presence of grandfather, papa, or the Veteran's wife or daughter. They would shake hands and gaze at each other. With unbearable intensity. On the other hand if she tried to go out alone and met him alone, then yes. And they would kiss and embrace to make up for all those years. And if he asked her, she would never go home. Because love is more important than anything else.

Grandmother had never been to the mainland, except to the small town where the spa was, and in spite of what her sister had written she thought that in Milan people would meet easily, as in Cagliari, and she was extremely excited because she thought she would see her Veteran on the street immediately. But Milan was very big, very tall, the buildings were massive, with sumptuous decorations; it was beautiful, gray and foggy, choked with traffic; bits of sky appeared amid the bare branches of the trees, and there were so many lighted shops, car headlights, traffic lights, clattering trams, crowds of people, their faces turned toward the collars of their coats in the rainy air. As soon as she got off the train in the Central Station, she looked closely at all the men to see if hers was there, tall, thin, the face gentle, carelessly shaved, the raincoat, because it was raining, and the crutch. There were so many men who got on and off those trains going everywhere, Paris, Vienna, Rome, Naples, Venice, and it was impressive how big and rich the world was, but he wasn't there.

Finally they arrived at the sister's street and her building; they had expected it to be modern, a kind of skyscraper, but instead it was old. Grandmother found it beautiful, even though the façade was crumbling and around the windows the ornamental stucco putti were missing their heads and the flowers their stalks, and the slats of the shutters and many pieces of the balcony balustrades had been replaced by wooden boards, many windowpanes by sheets of cardboard. The entrance was full of notices and the cards showing the names weren't under glass but pasted next to the only bell. Still, they were sure they had arrived, since the letters had gone back and forth for a year from that address in Milan. They rang and a woman leaned out from the balcony on the second floor. She said that the *sardignoli* women weren't home at that time, but they could come in and go up and ask some other *terún*, some other worthless southerners. And who were they? Were they looking for a servant? The *sardignole* women were the most reliable.

So they all went in. It was dark and the air was close, smelling of toilets and cabbage. The stairway must have been beautiful once, because the well in the middle was vast, but the bombing in the war would have damaged it, since many of the steps seemed dangerous. Grandfather insisted on going first, keeping to the wall, and then papa, holding tight to his hand, and then grandmother, whom he told to put her feet exactly where he had put his. They climbed up, all the way to the roof. There were no apartments. There was a doorway opening onto a long dark corridor that went all around the stairwell, with doors leading to storerooms. But to these storeroom doors were attached the cards with the names, and at the end was their brother-in-law's. They knocked, but no one answered; other people looked out into the corridor, and when they explained whom they were looking for, and who they were, the neighbors welcomed them warmly and invited them into their attic to wait. The brother-in-law was out with the rag cart, the sister at her cleaning job, the children stayed with the nuns all day. They sat on the bed, under the single window, through which a bit of gray sky was visible. Papa wanted to go to the bathroom, but grandfather glared at him, because it was clear that there was no bathroom.

Maybe they should have left right away. All they could bring those wretched people was shame. But it was late. They had already closely questioned the kind, affectionate neighbors, who were also from the south, and to leave now would have been to add insult to injury.

So they waited. The only one who was really sad was grandfather. Papa, at least, was enthusiastic, because in Milan he would find some scores that in Cagliari you had to order and wait months for, and grandmother didn't care about anything except meeting the Veteran: she had been waiting for this moment since the autumn of 1950. She immediately asked her sister where the *case di ringhiera* were, the buildings where the balconies ran all around the inside of the courtyard, with apartments opening off them. She said she was curious because she had heard about them, and so she got the directions for the neighborhood where they were concentrated. She let grandfather take papa to see La Scala, the Duomo, the Galleria Vittorio Emanuele, the Castello Sforzesco, and to buy the scores that could not be found in Cagliari. Of course grandfather was disappointed, but he said nothing, as always, and did not hinder her in any way. In fact, in the morning he showed her on the map the streets she had to take to see the places that interested her, and told her which tram she was to take and left her telephone tokens and useful numbers and money in case she got lost. She must not get upset; she was to call a taxi from a phone booth and return home quietly. Grandmother was not insensitive or stupid or mean, and she realized perfectly what she was doing and that she was hurting grandfather. This she would not have done for anything in the world. For anything in the world—except her love. So, with her heart in her throat, she went to look for the Veteran's house. She was sure that she would find it: a large, tall building with carved stone balconies, and a big door on the street and a passageway that formed a grand entrance and opened onto an enormous courtyard, facing which were the many stories of narrow balconies with railings. The Veteran was in that mezzanine apartment, with the door at the top of three or four steps, where his daughter waited for him in any weather, and windows with grates and two big rooms painted white, in which there was nothing of the past. Grandmother, with her heart in a turmoil, as if she were a criminal, went into a café and asked for a telephone book and looked for the name of the Veteran, but, even though he was from Genoa, there were pages of that name, and the only hope was to be lucky and find the right neighborhood and the right house. There were *case di ringhiera* on many long streets, and grandmother looked into the shops as well. They looked prosperous—the food shops resembled Vaghi, on Via Bayle, in Cagliari—and there were a lot of them, and they were crowded, but maybe the

Veteran, coming home from work, was doing the shopping; maybe she would see him in front of her, handsome in his raincoat when the rain fell on him. He would be smiling at her and telling her that he had not forgotten her, either, and in his heart had been expecting her.

Papa, the cousins, and grandfather, on the other hand, had gone into the center of the city, holding one another by the hand in the increasingly thick fog, and grandfather had bought his son and nephews chocolate at Motta, sitting at a little table, and then had taken them to the best toy stores, where he had bought his nephews Lego sets and little airplanes that fly above the ground, and even a home table-soccer game, and then they had gone into the Duomo and to have an ice-cream cone in the Galleria. My father speaks of that trip to Milan as a wonderful time except that he missed his piano. If grandmother had found the Veteran, she would have run away with him, just as she was, taking with her only what she had on, her new coat, her hair gathered under a wool beret, and her purse and the shoes she had bought so that if she met him she would look elegant.

Never mind about papa and grandfather, even though she loved them, and they would miss her terribly. She consoled herself with the idea that the two of them were a unit: they were always talking, a little ahead of her when the three of them went out, and at the table they chatted to each other while she washed the dishes, and when papa was little he wanted his father to say good night, and read him a bedtime story and give him all the reassurances that children need before going to sleep. Never mind about Cagliari, about the dark, narrow streets of Castello that unexpectedly opened to a sea of light, never mind about the flowers she had planted that would flood the terrace of Via Manno with color, never mind about the laundry hanging out in the mistral. Never mind about the beach at the Poetto, a long desert of white dunes beside clear water that, no matter how far you walked, never got deep, while schools of fish swam between your legs. Never mind about summers in the blue-and-white striped bathing hut, the plates of *malloreddus* with tomato sauce and sausage after swimming. Never mind about her village, with the odor of hearth fires, of pork and lamb and the incense in church when they went to her sisters' for holidays. But then the fog became denser and the top stories of the buildings seemed to be enveloped in clouds and you had to practically bump into people to see them, for they were mere shadows.

In the next days, in the city still shrouded in fog, grandfather took her by the arm, and on his other side held papa by the shoulders, who in turn gave his hand to the smaller cousins, so that, attached to one another, they would not get lost and could still enjoy the things that were close up and never mind those which the fog made invisible. A strange cheerfulness had come over grandfather, ever since grandmother had stopped looking for the *case di ringhiera*. He kept making jokes, and at meals they all laughed, and the attic didn't seem so squalid and cramped anymore. And when they went out, tied together like that, even grandmother, if she hadn't had that nearly heart-stopping longing for the Veteran, would have been amused by grandfather's jokes.

On one of those days he became obsessed with the idea that he had to buy her a nice dress, one that was worthy of a trip to Milan, and he said something he had never said before: "I want you to buy something beautiful. Really beautiful."

And so they stopped to look in all the finest shop windows, and papa and the cousins grumbled because it was very boring to wait while grandmother tried this and that for the mirror, indifferently.

By now, in fog-wrapped Milan, there was less and less likelihood of meeting the Veteran, and grandmother didn't care at all about the dress, but they bought it anyway, a paisley pattern in pastels, and grandfather insisted that she loosen her bun in the shop, to see what all those blue and pink moons and stars looked like with her cloud of black hair. He was so happy with the purchase that he wanted grandmother to wear the new dress every day under her coat, and before they went out he'd make her twirl around, and he'd say, "It's beautiful," but he seemed to mean "You're beautiful."

And for this, too, grandmother never forgave herself. For having been unable to seize those words out of the air and be happy.

When the moment came for goodbyes, she sobbed with her cheek against the suitcase, not for her sister, her brother-in-law, her nephews, but because if destiny hadn't willed her to see the Veteran, then it meant that he was dead. She remembered that in the autumn of 1950 she had believed she was in the Hereafter, and then he was so thin, and with his slender neck, his amputated leg, the childlike skin and hands, and that terrible eastward march and the concentration camp and the shipwrecks and the possibility that the father of his daughter was a Nazi—she felt that he was dead. If he hadn't been he would have looked for her, he knew where she lived, and Cagliari isn't Milan. Truly the Veteran must no longer be alive, and so she wept. Grandfather picked her up and sat her down on the only bed under the small attic window. He consoled her. He put a glass in her hand for a farewell toast and her sister and brother-in-law made a toast to meeting in better times, but grandfather didn't want to toast better times—he wanted to toast that very visit, when they had all been together and had eaten well and had some laughs.

Then grandmother, with the glass in her hand, thought that maybe the Veteran was alive—after all, he had survived so many terrible things, why shouldn't he make it in normal life? And she thought, too, that she still had an hour, with the tram ride to the Central Station, and the fog was lifting. But, when they reached the station, there was only a little time before the train left for Genoa, where they would get the boat and then another train; and life would begin again, where in the morning you water the flowers on the terrace and then make breakfast and then lunch and dinner, and if you ask your husband and son how things are going they answer, "Normal. Everything normal. Don't worry," and never tell you things, the way the Veteran did, and your husband never says that you're the only one for him, the one he was waiting for, and that in May of 1943 his life changed—never, in spite of the increasingly refined services in bed and all the nights you sleep there together. So now if God didn't want her to meet the Veteran let him kill her. The station was dirty, littered with trash and spit. While she sat and waited for her husband and son to get the tickets, because papa never chose to stay with her but preferred to stand in line with grandfather, she noticed a wad of gum stuck to the seat and smelled the odor of the toilets and felt an infinite disgust for Milan, which seemed to her terrible, like the whole world.

As she followed grandfather and papa, chattering to each other, up the escalator leading to the trains, she thought that if she turned back they wouldn't even realize it. The fog had cleared now. She would continue to look for the Veteran throughout all the disgusting streets of the world, despite the winter cold that was approaching; she would beg and maybe even sleep on benches, and if she died of tuberculosis or hunger so much the better.

She let go of her suitcases and packages and rushed down, crashing into all the people going up, saying "Excuse me, excuse me!" But right at the end she stumbled, and the escalator swallowed up a shoe and a piece of her coat and tore the beautiful new dress and her stockings and her woolen cap, which had fallen off, and the skin of her hands and legs, and she had cuts and scrapes all over. Two arms helped lift her up. Grandfather had run down after her, and now he was holding her and caressing her as he would have done with a child: "Nothing happened," he said to her, "nothing happened."

When they got home she started to do the laundry, all the dirty clothes from the visit, shirts, dresses, undershirts, socks, underwear: all the new things they had bought for the trip to Milan. They were doing well now, and grandmother had a Candy washing machine with two settings, for normal clothes and for delicates. She separated the clothes: those that were to be washed at a high temperature and those to be done in warm water. But maybe her thoughts were elsewhere, who knows, and she ruined everything. Papa told me that she hugged him and grandfather, amid sobs and tears, and got the knives from the kitchen and put them in their hands so that they could kill her; she scratched her face and beat her head against the wall and threw herself on the floor.

Later, my father heard grandfather telephoning the aunts and saying that, in Milan, she hadn't been able to stand seeing her younger, coddled sister reduced to such a state. Here in Sardinia the small landowners had been modest but dignified and respected, and now the failed agrarian reforms had ruined them, and they had had to emigrate, the women to be servants, which for a husband is the worst humiliation, the men to breathe the poisons of the factories, without protection and, above all, without respect, and in school the children were ashamed of their Sardinian last names, with all those "u"s. He himself had had no idea about this: the sister and brother-in-law had written that they were well and he had thought of surprising them by going to visit and instead it had been humiliating. The children had devoured the sausages and the prosciutto as if they hadn't eaten for goodness knows how long, and his brother-in-law, when he cut the cheese and opened the bottle of *mirto*, was moved, and had told him he could never forget that when the property was divided grandfather hadn't wanted grandmother's part, but, unfortunately, that had been wasted; for, while it had seemed to them that one couldn't live on the land, those who stayed had been right. Grandmother, who, as her sisters well knew, was made in her own way, couldn't stand this, and then today she had also learned that President Kennedy was shot in Dallas, and had ruined a load of laundry. He didn't care, money comes and goes, but there was no way to calm her and her son was upset. Could they please come to Cagliari, right away, on the first bus.

But then, for my great-aunt and uncle and cousins, things improved. They moved out of the attic to the sub-urb of Cinisello Balsamo, and my father, who always went to visit them when, as a musician, he was touring, said that they lived in a tall apartment building full of immigrants, in a complex of buildings for immigrants, but there was a bathroom and a kitchen and an elevator. At a certain point you couldn't speak of immigrants anymore, because they considered themselves Milanese, and no one called them *terún*, because now the fight was between the reds and the blacks in San Babila, where the cousins beat up their rivals and were beaten up by them, while papa went to the Giuseppe Verdi with his bags full of scores and had no interest in politics. Papa told me that arguments broke out between him and the cousins. About politics and about Sardinia. Because they asked stupid questions like: "Is that sweater made from *orbace*?"—of a beautiful heavy sweater knitted by grandmother of the coarse Sardinian wool. Or: "What kind of transportation do you have down there?" Or: "Do you have a bidet? Do you keep chickens on the balcony?"

So at first papa laughed, but then he got mad and said, Fuck you, even though he was a quiet, well-brought-up pianist. It was that they couldn't forgive his lack of inter-est in politics—he didn't hate the bourgeoisie enough, he had never hit a Fascist and had never been hit. They, still boys, had attended Capanna's rallies, had marched in Milan in May of 1969, had occupied the state school in 1971. But they all loved each other and always made up.

They had become friends in that November of 1963, in the attic, when they wandered over the rooftops, climbing out through the little window unbeknownst to their parents: the uncle of Milan who was out selling rags, with the uncle of Cagliari helping him; the aunt of Milan off cleaning for her rich people, and the aunt of Cagliari, completely mad, studying the architecture of the *case di ringhiera*, with that unforgettable woolen cap kept on by her hair, braided and rolled into chignons in the Sardinian style.

Grandmother told me that later her sister telephoned her from Milan to say that she was worried about papa, he was so out of the world, so engrossed in his music. He had no girlfriends, while her sons, who were younger, already did. The fact is that papa was never very with it: he had short hair when everyone wore it long except the Fascists, and he, poor guy, was certainly not a Fascist—it was that he didn't want his hair to get in his eyes when he played. She felt sorry for him, without a girlfriend, all alone with his scores. So grandmother, when she hung up, began to cry, fearful that she had transmitted to her son that kind of madness that puts love to flight. He had been a solitary child, whom no one invited anywhere, an unsociable child, at times awkwardly affectionate, whose company no one wanted. In the upper grades things had gone better, but not much. She tried to tell papa that other things existed in the world, and so did grandfather, though he laughed about it, and they couldn't forget the night of July 21, 1969, when, while Neil Armstrong walked on the Moon, their son had not interrupted his practicing of the Brahms Paganini Variationen Opera 35 Heft I, for the concert at the end of the semester.

12.

When grandmother realized she was old she told me that she was afraid of dying. Not of death itself, which was supposed to be like going to sleep or taking a journey, but she knew that she had offended God, because he had given her so many wonderful things in this world and she hadn't been happy, and for this God could not forgive her. All things considered, she hoped that she really was insane; if she was sane, Hell was certain. But she would discuss it with God, before she went to Hell. She would point out to him that if he creates a person in a certain way then he can't expect her to act as if she were not her. She had spent all her energy persuading herself that this was the best possible life, and not that other one, longing and desire for which took her breath away. But for certain things she would sincerely ask God's pardon: the paisley dress that grandfather had bought her in Milan and that she had torn in the escalator at the station; the cup of coffee placed at the foot of the bed, in their first year of marriage, like a dog's bowl; her inability to enjoy all those days by the sea, when she thought that the Veteran, so agile with his crutch, would arrive at the Poetto.

And the winter day when grandfather came home with a bag of mountain clothing, borrowed from somewhere or other, and proposed a trip up the Supramonte, which had been arranged by his office for the employees of the salt works, and she, even though she had never been to the mountains, had felt only an uncontainable irritation, and the sole wish to tear that ridiculous clothing out of his hands. But he stubbornly kept telling her that true Sardinians should know Sardinia.

For grandfather there was a pair of ugly sneakers and a heavy sweater, which was also very ugly; there were better things for her and the child. In the end grandmother reluctantly said "All right," and went to make sandwiches, while grandfather, who always helped her, for some reason, played a melancholy *plin-plin* on the piano of the Signorine Doloretta and Fanní. They went to bed early because they were to be at the meeting place at five in the morning. They were to go to Orgosolo and climb up to Punta sa Pruna, cross Foresta Montes, continue on to the megalithic circle of Dovilino and walk through the mountains that link Gennargentu to Supramonte, as far as Mamoiada. Everything was covered with snow and papa was beside himself with joy, but grandfather's teeth were already chattering, and others in the group advised the warm hearth and potato ravioli and *porchetto* on the spit and a local spirit, *fil'e ferru*, from a restaurant in the town. But he stubbornly refused. They had to become acquainted with the mountains of Sardinia, they who were people of the sea and the plain.

The Foresta Montes, one of the few virgin forests in Sardinia, whose ancient ilexes had never been cut down, was sunk in silence, and the soft white snow came up to the knees. So grandfather's shoes and pants were immediately soaked, but he kept going, without a word.

And he walked at the same pace as the others. Grandmother went on ahead for a good stretch, as if she had neither husband nor son, but when, down in the valley, the lake of Oladi appeared, frozen, as if it had dropped into that immense solitude from the world of fantasy, then she stopped to wait for them.

"Look! Look how beautiful it is!"

And when they crossed the oak wood, where the slender trunks were intertwined and covered with moss in the shape of snowflakes, she saved some of the fantastic leaves in her pocket and also picked a bunch of thyme, for making broth when they returned to Cagliari. And she stayed at his pace, her beautiful fur-lined shoes in step with those ugly ones of grandfather's, because she wasn't angry with him—on the contrary, she was so sorry she didn't love him. She was so sorry, and it pained her, and she wondered why God, when it comes to love, which is the principal thing, organizes things in such a ridiculous way: where you can do every possible and imaginable kindness, and there's no way to make it happen, and you might even be mean, as she was now, not even lending him her scarf, and yet he followed her through the snow, half frozen, missing the chance, lover of food that he was, to eat the local potato ravioli and *porchetto* on the spit. During the trip home she felt so sorry that in the darkness of the bus she leaned her head on his shoulder and sighed, as if to say "Ah well."

And she was frightened at how cold grandfather was, like someone frozen to death.

At home she made a hot bath and dinner and was scared by how much grandfather drank. It was the same as always, but it was as if she had never noticed.

That night, however, was wonderful. Better than ever

before. Grandmother had put papa to bed and, wearing an old bathrobe and slip, ready to go to sleep, was absent-mindedly eating an apple. Grandfather, locking the kitchen door to be sure that the child wouldn't come in, began the brothel game, ordering her to take off her bathrobe and slip and lie naked on the table, laid as if for his favorite meal. He turned on the heater, so that she wouldn't catch cold, and began to eat dinner again, helping himself to all those good things. He touched her and worked her all over, and, before tasting anything, even the delicious sausage from the village, he put it in grandmother's cunt—in the brothel, that's the word you have to use. She got extremely excited, and started touching herself, and, love him or not, at that moment nothing mattered anymore, all she wanted was to continue the game.

"I'm your whore," she moaned.

Then grandfather poured wine over her whole body and licked and sucked, especially her big buttery breasts, which were his passion. But he wanted to punish her, too, maybe for her behavior on the outing, or who knows, you could never understand grandfather, and, taking off his belt, he made her walk around the kitchen like a dog, hitting her but being careful not to hurt her too much and not to leave marks on her beautiful behind. Under the table grandmother caressed it and put it in her mouth, which by now she was expert at, but every so often she stopped to ask if she was a good whore, and how much she had earned; and she would have liked never to stop playing at the brothel.

They played for a long time and then grandfather got out his pipe, and she curled up on the opposite side of the bed and as usual fell sleep.

13

With the Veteran, on the other hand, the nights were so filled with emotion that—because she had found, surely, the famous principal thing—she stayed awake gazing at how handsome he was, taking advantage of some glow in the darkness; and when he started in fear, as if he heard shots, or because bombs were falling on the ship, breaking it in two, she touched him lightly with her finger, and the Veteran, in his sleep, responded by drawing her to him, so that he wasn't apart from her even when he was sleeping. Then grandmother boldly made a hollow for herself in the curve of his body and put the Veteran's arm around her shoulders and his hand on her head, and the impression made by this position, which she had never before experienced, was such that she couldn't resign herself to the idiotic—in her view—idea of sleeping when you're happy. So you had to wonder if lovers lived like that. And if it was possible. And if even they at a certain point had to decide to eat and sleep.

Now the Veteran had the black notebook with the red border, which he read, and he was a very demanding professor, because for every spelling mistake, or repetition of the same word, or other mistake, he gave her a spanking and mussed up her hair and insisted that she rewrite. "*Non mi va bééne*, I don't like it," he said with that narrow "e" of Genoa and Milan, but grandmother wasn't offended; in fact, she was highly amused. And she was wild about the music when he performed classical works with all the instruments, and then after a while he would do them again and she would guess the title and the composer; or he sang operas, with the voices of the men and the women. Sometimes he recited poems, for example those of a schoolmate of his, Giorgio Caproni, which grandmother loved, because she felt she was in Genoa, where she had never been, but it seemed to her that the places in the poems resembled Cagliari. Thus *vertical*, because when you arrive in the harbor from the sea—it had happened to her once, on a boat returning from Sant'Efisio—the houses look as if they were built on top of one another. Cagliari, like the Genoa described by the Veteran and his friend, or by that other unfortunate fellow, Dino Campana, who died in a mental asylum, is a *dark* and *labyrinthine* and *mysterious* and *damp* city, which has sudden and unexpected openings onto the great, blinding *Mediterranean light*. So, even if you're hurrying, you can't not look out over a wall, or an iron railing, can't not enjoy the *astonishingly rich* sky and sea and sun. And if you look down you see the roofs, the geranium-dotted terraces and the drying laundry, and the agave plants on the cliffs and the life of the people, which seems to you truly small and fleeting, yet also joyful.

Of grandmother's services the Veteran's favorite was the geisha, which was also the most difficult. With grandfather she managed it by telling him what they would have for dinner, but the Veteran wanted sophisticated routines like descriptions of the Poetto beach and of Cagliari and of her village, and stories of her daily life and her past and the emotions she had felt in the well, and he asked a lot of questions and wanted detailed answers. So my grandmother emerged from her silence and began to enjoy this, and she went on and on about the white dunes of the Poetto and their blue-and-white striped bathing hut, and how if you went there in winter, after a wind, to make sure it was still standing, mountains of white sand blocked the entrance, and if you looked from the shoreline it really was like a snowy landscape, especially if the cold was intense and you were wearing gloves and a wool cap and overcoat and all the windows of the huts were closed. Except that the huts had blue, or orange, or red stripes, and even though the sea was behind you, you certainly knew it was there. In summer they spent vacations there, along with the neighbors and their children, and brought everything they needed in a cart. She had a dress buttoned up the front, just for the seaside, with big embroidered pockets. When the men came, on Sunday or for their holidays, they wore pajamas or terrycloth bathrobes, and they all bought sunglasses, including grandfather, though he had always said that sunglasses made people give themselves airs—*ta gan'e cagai*.

How she loved Cagliari and the sea and her village, with its odor of wood, hearth, horse manure, soap, grain, tomatoes, warm bread.

But not as much as the Veteran. Him she loved above all else.

With him she felt no embarrassment, not even if they peed together to get rid of the stones, and since her whole life she had been told that she was like someone from the land of the moon, it seemed to her that she had finally met someone from her own land, and that was the principal thing in life, which she had never had.

In fact, after the thermal cure, grandmother never again scrawled over the decorations on the wall, which are still here in Via Manno, or tore the embroidery, which is still on the pockets of the smocks I wore as a child, and which, God willing, and I hope very much that he is, I will pass on to my children. My father's embryo did not lack the principal thing.

She had given the little notebook to the Veteran, because she wouldn't have time to write now. She had to begin to live. Because the Veteran was a moment and grandmother's life was many other things.

14

As soon as she came home she got pregnant, and in all those months she never had a kidney stone, and her stomach swelled, and grandfather and the neighbors wouldn't let her touch anything and treated her *cummenti su nènniri*, like a shoot of grain just emerged from the earth. My father had a cradle of blue-painted wood and a layette put together at the last moment, superstitiously, and when he was a year old grandfather wanted to have a big celebration in the kitchen at Via Sulis, with the hand-embroidered cloth on the table. He bought a camera, and finally, poor man, he tasted a truly happy birthday cake—American style, sponge cake with layers of custard and chocolate, and a candle. Grandmother isn't in the pictures. She had fled in tears to the bedroom, overcome by emotion, because they had begun to sing "Happy Birthday." And when they tried to persuade her to return, she kept saying she couldn't believe that a child had come out of her, and not just kidney stones. And she continued to weep uncontrollably, and her sisters, who had come from the village for the occasion, surely expected some *macchiòri*, some craziness, that would reveal to all those people that grandmother was mad. Instead, grandmother got up from the bed, dried her eyes, and went back to the kitchen and took her child in her arms. She isn't in the photographs because, with her eyes swollen, she felt ugly, and she wanted to be pretty for her son's first birthday.

Grandmother became pregnant other times, but all my father's possible siblings evidently lacked the principal thing, and turned back after the first months, unwilling to be born.

In 1954 they came to live on Via Manno. They were the first to leave the common house on Via Sulis, and even though Via Manno is just around the corner, they felt regret. So on Sundays grandfather invited the old neighbors and he grilled fish or sausages on the terrace and toasted bread with oil, and when the weather was good they put out picnic tables and chairs, which in summer they brought to the bathing hut on the Poetto. Grandmother loved Via Manno right away, even before it was built, ever since she had gone to see the hole and the mounds of rubble. The terrace soon became a garden. I remember the fox grape and ivy that climbed up the back wall, the geraniums grouped by color, violets, pinks, reds. In spring a little yellow forest of broom and freesias bloomed, in summer dahlias and fragrant jasmine and bougainvillea, and in winter the pyracantha had so many red berries that we used them as Christmas ornaments.

When the mistral blew we put on bandannas and hurried up to save the plants, setting them against the walls or covering them with plastic, while some of the more delicate ones we brought into the house until the wind stopped blowing, sweeping everything away.

15.

Sometimes I thought that the Veteran hadn't loved grandmother. He hadn't given her his address, and he knew where she lived and had never sent even a postcard; he could have signed it with a girl's name—grandmother would have recognized his handwriting because of the poems she had kept. The Veteran didn't want to see her again. He, too, thought she was mad and was afraid of finding her on the steps of his house one day, or in the courtyard, waiting in whatever weather, rain, fog, or dripping with sweat if it was one of those hazy windless summers in Milan. Or no. Maybe it really was love and he didn't want her to commit the folly of leaving for him all the things of her world. And then why show up and ruin everything? Appear and say, "Here I am, I'm the life that you could have lived and didn't." Torture her, poor woman. As if she hadn't suffered enough, up in the loft, cutting her arms and her hair, or in the well, or staring at the door on those Wednesdays. And to make a sacrifice of that kind, to stay away for the good of the other, you have to really love that person.

16

I wondered, without ever daring to say it to anyone, naturally, if the real father of my father was the Veteran, and when I was in the last year of high school and studying the Second World War and the professor asked if any of our grandfathers had fought, and where, my instinct was to say yes. My grandfather was a lieutenant on the heavy cruiser Trieste, III Division of the Royal Navy, and he took part in the inferno of Matapan in March, 1941, and was shipwrecked when the Trieste was sunk by the 3rd squadron of the 19th B17 Bomber Group, at the inlet of Mezzo Schifo, in Palau. That was the only time grandfather came to Sardinia, and he saw our sea when the waves were red with blood. After the Armistice the Germans imprisoned him on the light cruiser Jean de Vienne, captured by the Navy in 1942, and he was deported to the concentration camp of Hinzert and interned there until the Germans retreated to the east, in the winter of '44, in the deep snow and ice, and if you didn't march they shot you or split your head with a rifle butt. Luckily the Allies arrived and an American doctor amputated his leg. But my grandfather was still a very handsome man, as grandmother said, a man to look at secretly, in the first days at the baths, while he was reading, with that boyish neck bent over the book and those liquid eyes and that smile and those strong arms with the shirtsleeves rolled up and those hands, so large and childlike for a pianist—and to long for all the rest of your life. And longing is sad, but there's a trace of happiness in it, too.

17

Over the years grandmother began to have kidney problems again, and every two days I picked her up in Via Manno and took her to have dialysis. She didn't want to cause me any inconvenience, so she waited down in the street with her bag, which held a nightgown and slippers and a shawl, because she was always cold after the dialysis, even in summer. Her hair was thick and black and her eyes bright and she still had all her teeth, but her arms and legs were full of holes, because of the intravenous tubes, and her skin had turned yellowish and she was so thin that as soon as she got in the car and put the purse on her lap I had the impression that that object, which couldn't have weighed more than half a pound, might crush her.

One dialysis day she wasn't at the door, and I thought she must be feeling weaker than usual. I ran up the three flights of stairs, so we wouldn't be late, since the hospital had a strict schedule for the treatment. I rang but she didn't answer, and I was afraid that she had fainted, so I opened the door with my keys. She was lying peacefully on the bed, asleep, ready to go out, with her bag on the chair. I tried to wake her, but she wouldn't respond. I felt a desperation in my soul: my grandmother was dead. I picked up the telephone and I remember only that I wanted to call someone who would revive my grandmother, and it took a while to convince me that no doctor could do it.

Only after she died did I learn that my great-grandparents had wanted to commit her to a mental institution, and that before the war they had come from the village to Cagliari on the bus, and that the asylum, on Monte Claro, had seemed to them a good place for their daughter. My father never knew these things. My great-aunts told mamma, when she was about to marry papa. They invited her to the village, to speak to her in great secrecy and let her know what blood ran in the veins of the boy she loved and with whom she would have children. They were taking on this embarrassing situation because their brother-in-law—even though he had always known everything and, arriving as an evacuee in that month of May, had seen her *de dognia colori*, in every guise—had not had the proper manners to tell his future daughter-in-law a thing. They didn't want to criticize him, he was a fine man, and, though a Communist and an atheist and a revolutionary, for their family he had been *sa manu de Deus*, sacrificing to marry grandmother, who was ill *de su mali de is perdas, sa minor cosa, poita su prus mali fiara in sa conca*, with her kidney stones, the lesser evil—the greater was in her head. Because when grandmother was gone suitors came for them, too, poor women, and without that sister—who was often shut up in the hayloft, and cut her hair so she looked like a mangy dog—normal life had begun.

They could understand that he hadn't told his son, since the blood he had he already had, but she was a healthy girl, and it was right that she should know. So, sitting on the bench with the Sardinian sweets in front of her and coffee in the cups with the gilded edges, my mother listened to the story told by her future aunts.

The asylum had seemed to the parents a good place for grandmother; it was on a densely wooded hill where maritime pines, ailanthus, cypresses, oleanders, broom, and locusts grew, and there were paths grandmother could walk on. And then it wasn't a matter of a single large, grim structure that might frighten her but a series of villas built in the early years of the century, well tended and surrounded by gardens. The place where grandmother would have been was the ward for the Tranquil, a two-story villa with an elegant glass entrance, a living room, two dining rooms, and eight dormitories, and you wouldn't have known that crazy people lived there, except for the stairs, which were enclosed between two walls. Since grandmother was Tranquil, she would have been able to go out and perhaps go to the Administration building, which had a library and a reading room where she could write and read novels and poetry at her pleasure, but under control. And she would never have contact with the other villas, where the Agitated and the Semi-Agitated were, and terrible things would never happen to her, like being locked in an isolation cell or being tied to the bed. All in all, at home it was worse, because, when she had her crises of despair and wanted to kill herself, they had to save her somehow. And how, except by locking her up in the hayloft, where they had had to put in a barred window, or by tying her to the bed with rags. In the cottages at the asylum, on the other hand, the windows had no bars. They were of a type adopted by a Dr. Frank in the asylum in Musterlinger: they were provided with an old spring lock, and there was wire mesh in the glass, but it was invisible. The parents had taken the information packet for admission to the Cagliari Asylum, although they would still have to persuade grandmother to be examined, and they themselves needed to think about it. And then Italy entered the war.

But they couldn't keep her at home, and even if she had never hurt anyone, except herself and her things, and wasn't a danger, the people in the village always indicated their street by saying *inguni undi biviri sa macca*, there, where the crazy woman lives.

Grandmother had always embarrassed them, ever since the time when, in church, she had seen a boy she liked and kept turning toward the pews where the boys sat and smiled at him and stared at him and the boy giggled, too. She had taken the pins out of her hair, and let it loose, a shiny black cloud; it seemed the devil's weapon of seduction, a kind of witchcraft. My great-grandmother ran out of the church dragging the girl who was then her only daughter, and who was shouting, "But I love him and he loves me!" As soon as they got home she thrashed her, using whatever she could find—saddle girths, belts, pots, carpet beaters, ropes from the well—reducing the child to a doll that went limp in her hands. Then she called the priest to get the devil out of her body, but the priest gave her a blessing and said that she was a good child and there was not a trace of the devil in her. My great-grandmother told this story to everyone to apologize for her daughter, to let people know that she was mad but good, and that there was no danger at their house. But, just to be safe, she practiced some exorcism on her until she married grandfather. In a certain sense, grandmother's illness could be defined as a kind of love folly. An attractive man had only to cross the threshold of the house and smile at her, or simply look at her—and, since she was very beautiful, this could happen—and she would imagine that he was a suitor. She began to expect a visit, a declaration of love, a proposal of marriage, and she was always writing in that wretched notebook; they had looked for it in order to show it to a doctor at the asylum, but couldn't find it. Obviously no one ever came to ask for her hand, and she would wait and stare at the door and sit on the bench in the *lolla*, dressed in her best things, looking beautiful, because she really was, and smile fixedly, as if she understood nothing, as if she had arrived from the land of the moon. Then her mother had discovered that she wrote letters or love poems to those men, and that when she realized they would never return the drama began, and she screamed and threw herself on the ground and wanted to destroy herself and all the things she had made, and they had to tie her to the bed with the rags. In reality, she had no suitors, because no one in the village would have asked for grandmother in marriage, and you could only to pray God that, with the shame of a madwoman in the family, someone would want the other sisters.

In May of 1943, their brother-in-law, an evacuee, homeless, his grief for his wife still fresh, saw every side of her, and there was no need to explain anything to him, because for grandmother spring was the worst season. In the other seasons she was calmer: she planted seeds in the flower beds, worked in the fields, made bread and cross-stitch embroidery, scrubbed the tile floor of the *lolla*, fed the chickens and the rabbits, and petted them, and painted such beautiful decorations midway up the walls that she was called on to do them in other houses, to be ready by spring. My great-grandmother was so pleased to have her working for others all that time that she never asked them to pay her, and this the great-aunts thought was unfair. In the first days of the evacuation, grandfather, at dinner, with the soup in front of him, told them about the house on Via Manno, about the bombs and the death of his family, who had all gathered there on May 13th for his birthday. His wife had promised him a cake, and he was about to arrive when the air-raid alarm sounded. He had thought that he would find the family at the shelter under the Public Gardens, but none of them were at the shelter. That night, grandmother got up and ruined her cross-stitch embroideries, ripping them up; and her wall paintings, covering them with hideous splotches; and she scratched her face and body with prickly roses, so the thorns were everywhere, sticking even in her head. The next day, their future son-in-law had tried to talk to her, and, since she was locked in a stall reeking of manure, he spoke to her from the courtyard, through the wooden door, and told her that life is like that, that there are terrible things but also beautiful ones, such as, for example, the decorations and the embroidery she had done—why had she destroyed them? Grandmother, from inside, in the stench, had answered, strangely, "My things seem beautiful, but it's not true. They're ugly. I'm the one who should have died. Not your wife. Your wife had the principal thing that makes everything beautiful. Not me. I'm ugly. I'm meant to stay in the manure and the rubbish. I'm the one who should have died."

"And what, in your view, *signorina*, is this principal thing?" grandfather had asked. But nothing more was heard from the stall. And later, when she lost the babies in the first months of pregnancy, she said that she would not have been a good mother because she lacked the principal thing, and that her children were not born because they, too, lacked that thing, and so she shut herself up in her world of the moon.

At the end of the story, the future aunts accompanied mamma to the bus. As they waited for the bus, after handing her bags filled with sweets, sausages, and loaves of *civraxiu*, and caressing her long, smooth hair, which was the style then, they asked, just to change the subject, what she wanted to do in life.

"Play the flute," mamma answered.

Of course, but they meant as work, real work.

"Play the flute," my mother repeated.

My great-aunts looked at one another, and it was obvious what they were thinking.

Mamma told me these things after grandmother died. She kept them to herself and wasn't afraid of letting her mother-in-law, whom she loved, bring me up. In fact, she thinks we should be grateful to grandmother, because she took on herself all the disorder that might have touched papa and me. According to mamma, in fact, someone in a family has to take on the disorder, because life is like that, a balance between the two; otherwise, the world would grow rigid and stop. If at night we sleep without nightmares, if papa and mamma's marriage has always been free of bumps, if I'm getting married to my first boyfriend, if we don't have panic attacks and don't try to kill ourselves, or throw ourselves into garbage bins, or slash ourselves, it's thanks to grandmother, who paid for everyone. In every family there's someone who pays the tribute, so that the balance between order and disorder is maintained and the world doesn't come to a halt.

For example, my maternal grandmother, Signora Lia, wasn't bad. She had tried to put order into her life at all costs, without succeeding and in fact causing greater damage. She wasn't a widow and the reason mamma had the same last name was not that her father was a cousin. And the reason she had never gone to Gavoi was not that Gavoi is ugly and has no seacoast. Mamma had known all this since she was a child, but with other people Signora Lia insisted on the business of the cousin with the same last name, and so whenever they had to show identification she was terrified that whoever was looking at it would talk, and so they mustn't see too many people or be on friendly terms with anyone, and she had to give presents to the teachers, or the doctors, or anyone else who knew the truth, so that they wouldn't talk.

And when someone would mention a teenage mother, calling her an *egua*, a whore, Signora Lia also expressed herself with the same word and, when they got home, mamma would go to her room and cry.

But then mamma had her flute music, and my father, and nothing else mattered to her in the least. As soon as she started going with papa she changed families, because that was a real family and grandfather was the father she had never had. He picked spinach and wild asparagus for her in the countryside, and cooked mussels for her because she had an iron deficiency, and when he went to the spring at Dolianova, to get a supply of water for grandmother, who had kidney stones again, he made the rounds of the farms and got all kinds of healthy foods you couldn't find in the city, fresh eggs, bread baked in a wood-burning oven, fruit without pesticides. Sometimes mamma went with him and one day she got attached to a chick left without mother or brothers and sisters, and grandfather and grandmother let her take it home. So the rooster Niki also became one of the family: he was the only pet mamma ever had—just imagine animals in Signora Lia's house. When papa wasn't there, and papa never was there, grandfather took her everywhere in the car, and if she was late and it was dark, he sat, fully dressed, in the armchair, ready to go if necessary.

It wasn't true that grandmother Lia had left because Gavoi is an ugly town and she had never quarreled with her family.

Gavoi is a beautiful town, in the mountains. The houses are two or three stories tall, and are often attached, and some look as if they were hanging between two others, supported by a horizontal beam; below them are open, nearly dark courtyards, full of flowers, especially hydrangeas, which like shade and dampness. From certain points in the town you can see the lake of Gusana, which changes color many times a day, shifting from pink to powder blue, to red, and purple, and if you climb Monte Gonari and it's a clear day, you can see the Gulf of Orosei.

She had run away. At eighteen. Pregnant by a shepherd who had worked for her family. In the early fifties he had emigrated to the mainland, but he returned as soon as he learned of the agrarian reform and the Rebirth Plan, hoping that he might now be able to live well in Sardinia. He had a mainland wife, who was completely out of place, and some savings so that he could buy his own land and graze his sheep without paying rent.

The year of Signora Lia's flight was her senior year at the classical high school in Nuoro, where she was a very good student. In Cagliari she found a place as a maid and she took mamma, as a newborn, to the nuns. When her daughter got a little older, she started studying, so that she could finish that interrupted year and get her diploma. She studied at night, after she came home from work and mamma was asleep. She stopped being a maid and got an office job and even bought a house, ugly but clean and orderly, of which she was mistress. She was an oak. A rock of our granite. And she never complained about her life of ashes after that one spark. She had often told her daughter about it, because from childhood mamma wanted to know about her father. Rather than a fairy tale, she told her the story of that morning when she had missed the bus for Nuoro. At that hour the shepherd was leaving Gavoi for the countryside, and had found her there, at the bus stop, in tears, because she was a good girl even if something of a grind. He was a man of an intense and particular handsomeness, good and honest and intelligent, but unfortunately already married.

"Hello, *donna* Lia."

"Hello."

At dawn they crossed the wild solitary places, swept up in a whirlwind of folly, in which it seemed that happiness was possible. From then on *donna* Lia often missed the bus. She ran away without telling him she was pregnant, because she didn't want to ruin his world, that poor man with the mainland wife, so out of place in Gavoi that she seemed unable even to have children.

For her family Signora Lia left a letter in which she said not to worry, to forgive her, but she needed to go somewhere else, as far as possible, she couldn't bear Gavoi and Sardinia any longer, maybe the Côte d'Azur or the Ligurian Riviera, they knew how she always climbed Monte Gonari hoping for a view of the sea. At first she telephoned almost every day but didn't say where she was. The older sister, who had acted as a mother, because her mother had died when she was born, wept and said that her father was ashamed to go out and her brothers were threatening to search to the ends of the earth for her and kill her. She stopped telephoning. She closed off forever love, dreams, and especially—after getting her diploma, since she didn't have to study anymore—literature and any other form of artistic expression, and when mamma wanted to play the flute she accepted it only on condition that it remain a diversion, a distraction from the truly important things.

After the death of Signora Lia—she was still young, but her lymph glands had become as hard as rocks and her blood had turned to water; she wouldn't go out because she was ashamed of being seen with that kerchief on her head after the chemotherapy—mamma got it into her head to look for her father. Her mother would never tell her his name, but she came up with a plan so she could discover it for herself. Papa told her that it wasn't a good idea, there was no need to put order into things, better to go along with the universal confusion and play on it. But she was stubborn as a mule, and so one summer morning, early, to avoid the heat, they set out in search of my maternal grandfather. During the journey mamma kept saying *sciollori*, stupid things, such as she felt like a newborn in her father's arms, and she kept laughing, and she found Gavoi beautiful, better than all the places she had been for papa's concerts, Paris, London, Berlin, New York, Rome, Venice. Nowhere more beautiful than Gavoi.

They had prepared a routine in which they would say they were researchers who were doing a study and gathering testimony about the first wave of migration from Sardinia; mamma had a notebook and tape recorder and had even made herself a card with a false surname. They went into a café, a drugstore, a tobacconist's, where they asked a lot of suspicious-seeming questions, but their air of honesty was soothing and they were able to ask about the families of the landowners, the ones that had had shepherds. The wealthiest had been, and was still, grandmother Lia's. Her oldest sister now lived in the big house with her daughter and son-in-law and grandchildren; there was room for all of them. Mamma sat down on the stoop of a house opposite and couldn't stop gazing. It was one of the finest buildings in the town, a three-story granite structure, with a central section on the street facing her and two wings that faced upward-sloping side streets. The ground floor had twelve shuttered windows and a massive darkgreen wooden front door with brass hinges. The second floor had a grand French window, also closed, on the central balcony. The third was all windows, whose heavy embroidered curtains prevented one from seeing inside. Mamma continued to stare at the house and couldn't imagine her mother—who had always been so poor, with half her salary going to mortgage payments—inside that house, in that wealthy environment. On one of the two side wings of the building, on the upsloping street, was the service entrance, a gate, and, inside, a garden of dog roses, lemon trees, laurel, ivy, and red geraniums at the windows. On the steps were some toys, a dump truck, a doll in a carriage. Mamma stood, hypnotized, until papa said, "Let's go."

My great-aunt had been warned by the pharmacist. A maid opened the door, followed by two children, and she led them upstairs, where the mistress was waiting. The stairs were of dark polished stone, but the room where her aunt waited was luminous, with that French window opening onto the balcony. "These are my daughter's children," she said. "She leaves them with me when she goes to work."

Mamma had lost the power of speech. Papa performed his part and said that he was working with his colleague, here, at the Historical Institute of Cagliari, who was doing research for her thesis on the first wave of migration from Sardinia, in the fifties. Could she be so kind, given that her family surely had had shepherds, as to let them know of any who had gone to the mainland in that period and who could tell their stories?

My great-aunt was a beautiful woman, dark, slender, with regular features, hair gathered softly and low on her nape; she was elegantly dressed even though she was at home, and wore Sardinian earrings, the kind that look like buttons. The maid, still followed by the children, who showed off a collection of pails, rubber water wings, and bathing suits, and announced that next week they would be going to the beach, brought them coffee on a tray, with Sardinian breakfast pastries.

"*Pizzinnos malos*, you little scamps," the grandmother said, smiling tenderly, "leave the guests alone—they're here to study."

"One of our men went to work in Milan in 1951. He was a fine boy, who had been with us since he was a child. The others left later, in the sixties. However, he returned; he had bought some land and sheep."

"And where is he now?" mamma spoke for the first time.

"*Addolumeu*, poor man," my great-aunt answered. "He threw himself down a well. He had a wife from the mainland, who had no children, and didn't even mourn him. After the tragedy she went back to the north."

"When?" papa asked, in a faint voice.

"In 1954. I remember very well, because it was the year my sister Lia died, the baby of the family."

And she pointed to a photograph on the credenza of a young girl with a romantic expression, next to a vase of fresh flowers.

"Our poetess," she added. And from memory she recited some lines:

My hope wakens, anguished,
In the blue bursts of spring
After withdrawing, ashamed,
In winter's pale light.
My hope can't understand you
And can't be understood
amid the sweet trembling yellow
Of the brash mimosas.

A love poem kept in the drawer, no one knows whom she was thinking of, poor child.

Mamma didn't say a word until Cagliari and finally papa asked, "Do you think he killed himself for your mother? Isn't it incredible that as a girl she wrote poems?"

Mamma shrugged, as if to say, "What do I care," or "How should I know?"

19

I came here to Via Manno today to clean up, because as soon as the work is finished I'm going to be married. I'm glad that the façade is being redone; it's been crumbling. The work was entrusted to an architect who's something of a poet and respects the building's past. This is its third incarnation: the first time, in the nineteenth century, it was narrower, and had just two balconies on each floor, with wrought-iron balustrades, and very tall windows, with two rows of three panes in the upper part and slats below; the big front door was surmounted by a stuccoed arch, and the roof was partly a terrace, then, too, and from the street you could see only the imposing cornice. Our apartment has been empty for ten years; we haven't sold or rented it, because we love it, and don't care about anything else. But then it hasn't really been empty. On the contrary.

When my father returns to Cagliari he comes here to play his old piano, the one that came from the Signorine Doloretta and Fanní.

He did that even before grandmother died, because mamma has to practice the flute, and so at home they always had to set a schedule. Papa took his scores and came here, and grandmother began cooking all the things he liked, but then, when it was time to eat, we'd knock at the door and he'd answer, "Thank you, later, later. You start." But I don't remember that he ever came to the table. He left the room only to go to the bathroom and if he found it occupied, for example by me—slow about everything, imagine in a bath—he would get angry, he who was such a quiet man, and say that he had come to Via Manno to practice and instead not a thing went as it should. When hunger, unscheduled, made itself felt violently, he went to the kitchen, where grandmother used to leave him a covered plate and a double boiler on the stove so he could warm up the food. He ate alone, drumming on the table with his fingers as if he were playing scales, and if, perhaps, we stuck our heads into the kitchen to ask him something, he responded in monosyllables, to make us go away, and be left in peace. The best was always to be in mid-concert; it's not everyone who gets to eat, sleep, go to the bathroom, do homework, watch television without sound while a great pianist plays Debussy, Ravel, Mozart, Beethoven, Bach, and the rest. And even if at grandmother's we were more comfortable when papa didn't come, it was wonderful when he was there, and as a child I always wrote something in honor of his presence—an essay, a poem, a story.

This house also didn't stay empty because I come here with my boyfriend. I always think that it still has grandmother's energy, and that if we make love in a bed in Via Manno, in this magical place with only the sound of the port and the cries of the seagulls, then we'll love each other forever. Because in love, perhaps, in the end you have to trust magic—it's not as if you can find a rule, something to follow to make things go well, like the Commandments.

*

And rather than do the cleaning, or read the news about the situation in Iraq, where it's not clear if those Americans are liberators or occupiers, I wrote, in the notebook that I always carry with me, about grandmother, the Veteran, his father, his wife, and his daughter; about grandfather, my parents, the neighbors of Via Sulis, my great-aunts, paternal and maternal, grandmother Lia, and the Signorine Doloretta and Fanní; about music, Cagliari, Genoa, Milan, Gavoi.

Now that I'm getting married the terrace is a garden again, as it was in grandmother's time. The ivy and the fox grape climb up the wall at the back and there are the groups of geraniums, red, violet, and white, and the rose-bush and the broom, which is thick with yellow flowers, and honeysuckle and freesias, dahlias and fragrant jasmine. The workers have waterproofed it and the dampness in the ceilings no longer causes bits of plaster to fall down on your head. They've also whitewashed the walls, leaving intact grandmother's decorations halfway up, of course.

That's how I found the famous black notebook with the red border and a yellowed letter from the Veteran. In fact I didn't find them. A worker gave them to me. A section of the living-room wall had flaked off, along with the decorations. Let's give it up, I said to myself, replaster it and put a piece of furniture in front of it. Grandmother had dug a hole at that point and hidden her notebook and the Veteran's letter, and then painted over it, but she didn't do a good job and the decorations disintegrated.

20

D ear *signora*," the letter from the Veteran says, "I am flattered and perhaps slightly embarrassed for all that you imagined and wrote about me. You ask me to evaluate your story from the literary point of view, and you apologize for the love scenes that you invented and also, above all, for the true things you wrote about my life. You say it seems to you that you have stolen something from me. No, my dear friend, to write of someone as you have done is a gift. For me you needn't worry about anything; the love that you invented between us moved me, and, as I read, excuse the audacity, I almost regretted that that love wasn't really there. But we talked so much. We kept each other company, and even had some laughs, unhappy as we were, there at the baths, isn't it true? You and those children who refused to be born, I and my war, the crutches, the suspicions. So many stones inside. You tell me that you became pregnant again as soon as you returned from the treatments, that you are hopeful again. I send you good wishes with all my heart, and I like to believe that I helped you get rid of the stones and that our friendship in some way helped you regain your health and the possibility of having children. You also helped me: my relations with my wife and child have improved, I'm managing to forget. But there is something else. And I imagine that you'll laugh when you read what I'm about to tell you: I'm not so sloppy as I was a few months ago at the spa. I'm through with sandals and wool socks, T-shirts and wrinkled trousers. You invented me with that beautiful starched white shirt and the shoes that were always polished, and I was pleased by that. I was really like that once. In the Navy you're in trouble if you're not always in perfect order.

"But to return to your story. Never stop imagining. You're not mad. Don't ever believe anyone who tells you a thing so unjust and spiteful. Write."

Milena Agus was a finalist for the Strega and Campiello prizes, and was awarded the prestigious Zerilli-Marimò prize for *Mal di pietre* (*From the Land of the Moon*), which went on to become an international bestseller. Agus lives in Cagliari, Sardinia.

Europa Editions publishes in the US and in the UK. Not all titles are available in both countries. Availability of individual titles is indicated in the following list.

Carmine Abate
Between Two Seas
"A moving portrayal of generational continuity."
—*Kirkus*
224 pp • $14.95 • 978-1-933372-40-2 • Territories: World

Salwa Al Neimi
The Proof of the Honey
"Al Neimi announces the end of a taboo in the Arab world:
that of *sex!*"
—*Reuters*
144 pp • $15.00 • 978-1-933372-68-6 • Territories: World

Alberto Angela
A Day in the Life of Ancient Rome
"Fascinating and accessible."
—*Il Giornale*
392 pp • $16.00 • 978-1-933372-71-6 • Territories: USA & Canada

Muriel Barbery
The Elegance of the Hedgehog
"Gently satirical, exceptionally winning and inevitably bittersweet."
—Michael Dirda, *The Washington Post*
336 pp • $15.00 • 978-1-933372-60-0 • Territories: USA & Canada

Gourmet Rhapsody
"In the pages of this book, Barbery shows off her finest gift: lightness."
—*La Repubblica*
176 pp • $15.00 • 978-1-933372-95-2 • Territories: World (except UK, EU)

Stefano Benni
Margherita Dolce Vita
"A modern fable...hilarious social commentary."—*People*
240 pp • $14.95 • 978-1-933372-20-4 • Territories: World

Timeskipper
"Benni again unveils his Italian brand of magical realism."
—*Library Journal*
400 pp • $16.95 • 978-1-933372-44-0 • Territories: World

Romano Bilenchi
The Chill
120 pp • $15.00 • 978-1-933372-90-7 • Territories: World

Massimo Carlotto
The Goodbye Kiss
"A masterpiece of Italian noir."
—*Globe and Mail*
160 pp • $14.95 • 978-1-933372-05-1 • Territories: World

Death's Dark Abyss
"A remarkable study of corruption and redemption."
—*Kirkus* (starred review)
160 pp • $14.95 • 978-1-933372-18-1 • Territories: World

The Fugitive
"[Carlotto is] the reigning king of Mediterranean noir."
—*The Boston Phoenix*
176 pp • $14.95 • 978-1-933372-25-9 • Territories: World

(with Marco Videtta)
Poisonville
"The business world as described by Carlotto and Videtta
in *Poisonville* is frightening as hell."
—*La Repubblica*
224 pp • $15.00 • 978-1-933372-91-4 • Territories: World

Francisco Coloane
Tierra del Fuego
"Coloane is the Jack London of our times."—Alvaro Mutis
192 pp • $14.95 • 978-1-933372-63-1 • Territories: World

Giancarlo De Cataldo
The Father and the Foreigner
"A slim but touching noir novel from one of Italy's best writers
in the genre."—*Quaderni Noir*
144 pp • $15.00 • 978-1-933372-72-3 • Territories: World

Shashi Deshpande
The Dark Holds No Terrors
"[Deshpande is] an extremely talented storyteller."—*Hindustan Times*
272 pp • $15.00 • 978-1-933372-67-9 • Territories: USA

Helmut Dubiel
Deep in the Brain: Living with Parkinson's Disease
"A book that begs reflection."—*Die Zeit*
144 pp • $15.00 • 978-1-933372-70-9 • Territories: World

Steve Erickson
Zeroville
"A funny, disturbing, daring and demanding novel—Erickson's best."
—*The New York Times Book Review*
352 pp • $14.95 • 978-1-933372-39-6 • Territories: USA & Canada

Elena Ferrante
The Days of Abandonment
"The raging, torrential voice of [this] author is something rare."
—*The New York Times*
192 pp • $14.95 • 978-1-933372-00-6 • Territories: World

Troubling Love
"Ferrante's polished language belies the rawness of her imagery."
—*The New Yorker*
144 pp • $14.95 • 978-1-933372-16-7 • Territories: World

The Lost Daughter
"So refined, almost translucent."—*The Boston Globe*
144 pp • $14.95 • 978-1-933372-42-6 • Territories: World

Jane Gardam
Old Filth
"Old Filth belongs in the Dickensian pantheon of memorable characters."
—*The New York Times Book Review*
304 pp • $14.95 • 978-1-933372-13-6 • Territories: USA

The Queen of the Tambourine
"A truly superb and moving novel."—*The Boston Globe*
272 pp • $14.95 • 978-1-933372-36-5 • Territories: USA

The People on Privilege Hill
"Engrossing stories of hilarity and heartbreak."—*Seattle Times*
208 pp • $15.95 • 978-1-933372-56-3 • Territories: USA

The Man in the Wooden Hat
"Here is a writer who delivers the world we live in…with memorable and moving skill."—*The Boston Globe*
240 pp • $15.00 • 978-1-933372-89-1 • Territories: USA

Alicia Giménez-Bartlett
Dog Day
"Delicado and Garzón prove to be one of the more engaging sleuth teams to debut in a long time."—*The Washington Post*
320 pp • $14.95 • 978-1-933372-14-3 • Territories: USA & Canada

Prime Time Suspect
"A gripping police procedural."—*The Washington Post*
320 pp • $14.95 • 978-1-933372-31-0 • Territories: USA & Canada

Death Rites
"Petra is developing into a good cop, and her earnest efforts to assert her authority…are worth cheering."—*The New York Times*
304 pp • $16.95 • 978-1-933372-54-9 • Territories: USA & Canada

Katharina Hacker
The Have-Nots
"Hacker's prose soars."—*Publishers Weekly*
352 pp • $14.95 • 978-1-933372-41-9 • Territories: USA & Canada

Patrick Hamilton
Hangover Square
"Patrick Hamilton's novels are dark tunnels of misery, loneliness, deceit, and sexual obsession."—*New York Review of Books*
336 pp • $14.95 • 978-1-933372-06-8 • Territories: USA & Canada

James Hamilton-Paterson
Cooking with Fernet Branca
"Irresistible!"—*The Washington Post*
288 pp • $14.95 • 978-1-933372-01-3 • Territories: USA & Canada

Amazing Disgrace
"It's loads of fun, light and dazzling as a peacock feather."
—*New York Magazine*
352 pp • $14.95 • 978-1-933372-19-8 • Territories: USA & Canada

Rancid Pansies
"Campy comic saga about hack writer and self-styled 'culinary genius' Gerald Samper."—*Seattle Times*
288 pp • $15.95 • 978-1-933372-62-4 • Territories: USA & Canada

Seven-Tenths: The Sea and Its Thresholds
"The kind of book that, were he alive now, Shelley might have written."
—*Charles Spawson*
416 pp • $16.00 • 978-1-933372-69-3 • Territories: USA & Canada

Alfred Hayes
The Girl on the Via Flaminia
"Immensely readable."—*The New York Times*
164 pp • $14.95 • 978-1-933372-24-2 • Territories: World

Jean-Claude Izzo
Total Chaos
"Izzo's Marseilles is ravishing."—*Globe and Mail*
256 pp • $14.95 • 978-1-933372-04-4 • Territories: USA & Canada

Chourmo
"A bitter, sad and tender salute to a place equally impossible to love
or leave."—*Kirkus* (starred review)
256 pp • $14.95 • 978-1-933372-17-4 • Territories: USA & Canada

Solea
"[Izzo is] a talented writer who draws from the deep, dark well of noir."
—*The Washington Post*
208 pp • $14.95 • 978-1-933372-30-3 • Territories: USA & Canada

The Lost Sailors
"Izzo digs deep into what makes men weep."—*Time Out New York*
272 pp • $14.95 • 978-1-933372-35-8 • Territories: World

A Sun for the Dying
"Beautiful, like a black sun, tragic and desperate."—*Le Point*
224 pp • $15.00 • 978-1-933372-59-4 • Territories: World

Gail Jones
Sorry
"Jones's gift for conjuring place and mood rarely falters."
—*Times Literary Supplement*
240 pp • $15.95 • 978-1-933372-55-6 • Territories: USA & Canada

Matthew F. Jones
Boot Tracks
"A gritty action tale."—*The Philadelphia Inquirer*
208 pp • $14.95 • 978-1-933372-11-2 • Territories: USA & Canada

Ioanna Karystiani
The Jasmine Isle
"A modern Greek tragedy about love foredoomed and family life."
—Kirkus
288 pp • $14.95 • 978-1-933372-10-5 • Territories: World

Swell
"Karystiani movingly pays homage to the sea and those who live from it."
—La Repubblica
256 pp • $15.00 • 978-1-933372-98-3 • Territories: World

Gene Kerrigan
The Midnight Choir
"The lethal precision of his closing punches leave quite a lasting mark."
—Entertainment Weekly
368 pp • $14.95 • 978-1-933372-26-6 • Territories: USA & Canada

Little Criminals
"A great story...relentless and brilliant."—*Roddy Doyle*
352 pp • $16.95 • 978-1-933372-43-3 • Territories: USA & Canada

Peter Kocan
Fresh Fields
"A stark, harrowing, yet deeply courageous work of immense power and magnitude."—*Quadrant*
304 pp • $14.95 • 978-1-933372-29-7 • Territories: USA & Canada

The Treatment and the Cure
"Kocan tells this story with grace and humor."—*Publishers Weekly*
256 pp • $15.95 • 978-1-933372-45-7 • Territories: USA & Canada